PRAISE FOR
THE PIANO STUDENT

"Carefully researched and explosively passionate, this story of forbidden love and unmet potential is not just for fans of Vladimir Horowitz or the piano, but for anyone who's ever felt the ineffable power of music."

—AJA GABEL,
author of *The Ensemble*

"With the complexity of a Russian piano concerto, Lea Singer has evoked the passionate love between the maestro Horowitz and the young man who became his student. She has richly imagined their forbidden relationship, which was marked by the same push-pull phrasing in the Chopin Nocturnes Horowitz often played, and that haunted them both for the rest of their lives."

—CHRIS CANDER,
author of *The Weight of a Piano*

"This intriguing, quirky novel, based on unpublished letters of Horowitz to a Swiss student, explores his hidden European years between living in Russia and the United States, and his hidden homosexual life outside his marriage with Wanda Toscanini."

—STEPHEN HOUGH, concert pianist and author of
*Rough Ideas: Reflections on Music and
More* and *The Final Retreat: A Novel*

"One of the greatest pianists of the last century, an illicit love affair with a young man, and a story using the genuine correspondence that passed between them—it makes for an utterly compelling read."

—JEREMY NICHOLAS,
author of *The Great Composers and Chopin: His Life and Music*

"A tender psychological depiction of an impossible love—and between the lines a good deal of veneration for the pianist Horowitz and for the persuasive power of music."

—*SÜDDEUTSCHE ZEITUNG*

"Lea Singer's novel combines narrative imagination and accurate research ... recounting vividly as well as exemplarily the multi-faceted history of a forbidden love between men and thereby captivating the reader."

—*WELTWOCHE*

"A book that tells with empathic devotion of music and death ... the story of a search for freedom in the most adverse circumstances ... The book poses the biggest question of all about relationships, What is true and what is a lie?"

—*NEUE ZÜRCHER ZEITUNG*

THE
PIANO
STUDENT

LEA SINGER

TRANSLATED FROM THE GERMAN BY
ELISABETH LAUFFER

NEW VESSEL PRESS
NEW YORK

New Vessel Press

www.newvesselpress.com

First published in German as *Der Klavierschüler*
Copyright © 2019 by Kampa Verlag AG, Zurich, Switzerland
Translation copyright © 2020 Elisabeth Lauffer

Financial support for the translation provided by a grant from the Kunststiftung NRW / Arts Foundation of North Rhine-Westphalia.

Library of Congress Cataloging-in-Publication Data
Singer, Lea
[Der Klavierschüler, English]
The Piano Student/Lea Singer; translation by Elisabeth Lauffer
p. cm.
ISBN 978-1-939931-86-3
Library of Congress Control Number 2020935330

I. Switzerland—Fiction

THE PIANO STUDENT

I

WE SHOULD STOP talking about him, the man in the passenger seat said as he opened the car door, or we'll have trouble carrying out the assignment.

You're right, the man behind the wheel agreed. We should stop.

They then stood by the vehicle, one to the right, the other to the left, and looked at the house below, his house. It sat directly on the water on the sunny side of Lake Zurich, about halfway down, in the district of Meilen. The lake sprawled out, motionless, and the trees were bare, wiped clean of color from warmer months. It was dry and not exactly bright, but blindingly pristine; neither man could look away.

Orson Welles would invite friends to watch his lover Rita Hayworth as she slept in his bed, said the man on the driver's side. Asleep, naked, messy hair, no makeup. He wanted the beauty of his possession to leave them speechless, and it did. Every last one was consumed with envy. They all desired what he had.

So what good did it do? the passenger asked.

For who? You talking about Orson Welles or him?

Him. As far as I know, Orson Welles died of natural causes.

They stared silently at the lake and the house on the shore, its inland side a striated bastion of travertine and granite. They had spent a long two and a half hours driving through road spray from Ascona, their last assignment, two and a half hours dedicated to him. They knew the route his life had taken, as though they had traveled it by streetcar daily, getting out at every stop. But there were no tracks. There was a starting point, but no destination. He'd been fleeing his whole life, he'd once said. It didn't appear that way from the outside. Reto Donati's ascent was one for the books. Its trajectory went from the very bottom straight to the very top, without the slightest hitch. Born to dirt-poor parents who, like others from Ticino, moved here in search of work following the war and were known derogatorily as chestnut roasters. One-and-a-half-room apartment with combination kitchen-bath in Zurich's fourth district, Kreis 4, toilet off the stairs, mother a seamstress, father a gardener. From there to star law student, cultured diplomat, and now presumptive frontrunner for the highest position on Switzerland's Federal Supreme Court.

The two men tugged at their gray jackets in unison. They straightened their ties in unison. Their shirts were both the color of blue skies in March, though they hadn't planned it. Then, at the same time, each touched his right hand to his left breast pocket. The driver could feel his standard equipment. The passenger could feel the thumb-sized vial. Brown glass, white plastic cap, white label. Pentobarbital sodium.

Water-soluble powder. Available only to physicians. Store at room temperature away from light.

It contained enough to kill three people.

With a glance over the roof of the car, the men caught each other trembling. Four ears could hear what neither would say.

Why are you so nervous?

Both were experienced. They knew it ran like clockwork. It always took thirty to thirty-five minutes. No one had ever refused to empty the vial. Some hesitated, others steeled themselves with a line, like, Okay, let's go.

But his case was different. Did that explain their hesitation? It wasn't sympathy hampering them. Sympathy had no place in their line of work; they left that to family members, provided there were any. Their imperative as executors, in fact, was to prevent the slightest hint of sympathy from creeping into their work. Failure to do so would discredit their entire organization.

On paper, all conditions had been met for carrying out the job.

He was fully conscious of his decision and was by no means acting on impulse.

It was entirely his choice.

There were no third parties who may have influenced him.

His motivation was different from the others', though. On the surface it appeared the same, but it lacked substance, the tangible heft underneath it all.

* * *

The sound of a grandfather clock striking the hour escaped the house. They were familiar with the clock, an heirloom from the Ticino grandparents—or really, the great-grandparents—not nice, just old, a desperate attempt at hominess, something the man of the house had otherwise spurned. The chimes were clearly audible; there must have been a window open. The men set out as the clock struck eleven. They descended the stairs through the garden side by side, their steps echoing the rhythm of the faded sound. It was a Japanese garden, its gravel and moss and creeping, crippled conifers at odds with the surroundings.

As the passenger placed his finger on the chrome button by the front door, he noticed it was ajar. Was he trying to make things easier for them? Or for himself? Was he trying to speed up the process?

It smelled unoccupied. I don't like being here. This would be easier for me in Venice, he had said.

The men didn't care about that, nor could they afford to. It was here, on Swiss soil, that the world traveler had to die, otherwise it could spell trouble. Not just for the two of them, but for their organization as a whole, which, in the four years since its founding, had handled every last case flawlessly and with the utmost discretion.

They were familiar with the house from their previous visit. It was a fastidiously maintained house that knew neither clutter nor dirt nor wear.

The naked black table gleamed in the middle of the dining room. The bedroom door was halfway open. The bed yawned, white and unoccupied. The living room was like a designer furniture exhibition, without any trace of life on the white leather.

The men could have saved themselves the trouble of opening the remaining twenty doors and peering into the remaining twenty rooms. As they opened the first three or four, they were haunted by the prospect of discovering his corpse dangling from the ceiling, sprawled on the floor by a bloodstained wall, or bobbing in red bathwater. Something inside them soon realized he wasn't there. Whether he'd absconded or been abducted—and more importantly, how it had happened and where he was now—was impossible to determine at first glance. No message, no suicide note, no sign of intruders.

Even his cars had a view of the lake. The men could see through the garage window that the two vehicles parked there were dry, the winged emblems above the radiator grilles freshly polished.

They went back inside. Surely they could find some evidence of what had changed so unexpectedly in the euthanasia candidate's life. They would have considered it tasteless to refer to him as such; working for an organization called Ars M. implied certain standards. One spoke of clients.

They searched the entire house, but discovered nothing that might reveal the candidate's whereabouts. All that remained was a question neither had ever encountered:

Should they lock the door behind them? Doing so would restrict their own access for further research.

Who, outside their group, was bound to detect his disappearance? He had fired his household staff, they knew, and he didn't have siblings, a wife, or children. Reproduction, he had said, had always seemed absurd to him.

Should they notify the police? They, of all people.

It was the one who had sat in the passenger seat who finally noticed it, on their third or fourth sweep of the house. The men's persistence was lost on this place. Nooks and hiding spots didn't exist here. Even the books—mostly heavy art books—stood at attention, arranged by height at precisely the same distance from the edge of the shelf. The vinyl collection was no different. It was only then, on the final look around, that the passenger noticed the black record on the turntable in the living room. The sleeve was propped against the wall behind it.

Kinderszenen, Opus 15 by Robert Schumann. The first movement was called "Of Foreign Lands and Peoples." The movement halfway through, No. 7, was marked with an *X*. "Träumerei," or "Dreaming," in F Major. 3:01 was printed beside it. The total running time of the *Kinderszenen* was 17 minutes, 41 seconds. Too brief, he thought.

The men silently walked out the door, letting it lock behind them, passed through the garden, and set out for Zurich. It wasn't until the car came to a stop in traffic outside the city that a groan escaped the passenger's body.

I'm actually glad, he said.

There will be a lot of dumb questions, the driver replied.

Yeah, but still. I had a weird feeling about this one.

Me too, the driver said and thought of the papers in his left breast pocket.

He watched as a right hand checked off little boxes in blue ink to confirm that all essential criteria had been evaluated. *Client exhibits: Sound judgment*, check. *Deliberation*, check. *Autonomy*, check. *Consistent expression of desire*, check. *Personal agency*, check. He then saw the way the hand hesitated to check off the three boxes—or even one of the three—on the following page: *Client can verify: Hopeless prognosis, Unbearable affliction*, or *Severe disability*.

It's known as the Sickness unto Death, the forty-five-year-old had said. That's its official designation. Forget scruples. You're helping me exit with dignity, just like the others.

When the client noticed that the hand completing the form was still hesitating, he closed his eyes and began to speak. In a very matter-of-fact way, his voice steady, cadence monotone, he described his remaining options.

Option 1: jump from the cathedral tower, like his father. Worst case scenario, kill others in the fall who didn't want to die. Best case scenario, wind up plastered to the pavement, a pulp of splintered bone and flesh. Option 2: procure and ingest the poison himself, which involved considerable risk of rescue, like his mother, who, following her husband's death, had vegetated for another three years, unable to use

LEA SINGER

her hands, a facility required to drain the liberating cocktail, as per their criterion for *personal agency*.

Option 3: hang himself from a rafter, like his uncle, and forever scar those who found him with the indelible image of his engorged tongue and purple face.

A check was placed next to *Hopeless prognosis* and a note added: *Major depression resistant to treatment. Likely hereditary / see attached.* The attachment included a psychiatric report detailing the standard antidepressants tested on this patient, all without success.

Back in Zurich, they called an emergency meeting. Two hours later, in the name of the Ars M. Agency for Assisted Suicide, the passenger alerted local police and the municipal administration in Meilen. Three hours later, in the presence of a notary public, police detective, and public prosecutor, he broke the seal on the missing man's will. The sole heir was a man with a Turkish name, who lived in Berlin. He could make no claim to the inheritance until the death had been recorded. That much was clear. That, and nothing else.

The assembled council asked the now-unemployed agents if they had investigated the three suicides in the man's family. The men exchanged another look, trembling as they had when their eyes locked over the roof of the car.

It took only a few hours to discover that his father had died peacefully four years earlier, at age 81, in a Catholic nursing home, where his mother had also died, also peacefully, two years later, at age 72, and that his only uncle had died in the 1970s, in a car crash in southern Italy.

The psychiatrist, who was also a psychoanalyst, confirmed that Reto Donati had been a patient of his and received psychotropic medication for chronic depression. No, he would not comment on the causes, particularly in light of the fact that the patient's passing was not yet confirmed.

The terminated housekeeper proved more cooperative. I'll tell you why I got fired, if you're curious: it was because of her. He was very hush-hush about it, but he was going to get married. Where did he—? Oh, in the classifieds. No, just a few weeks ago. It was because of the campaign. Running as a conservative without a wife, you know...

II

❧•❧

THE RESIDENTS OF KREIS 4, Zurich's fourth district, were bound by superstition. It was the one thing they had in common: everyone here believed in miracles, presumably because they had no other choice, as sooner or later the idea of earthly justice went out the window. The only reason superstition hadn't landed in the trash, among millions of condoms, soggy roaches, bottle caps, fake fingernails, spaghetti table scraps, and grimy sponges, was because of the guardian angels. These angels weren't floating in the ether. They were living the miracle known as success, right there among their neighbors in the Fourth. Like the guy who started out as a sneakered orderly in a locked psych ward, only to emerge as a darling of high fashion with his hand-printed silks; or the artists who once picked cigarette butts off the street, whose paintings were now considered investments; or the one-time waiters who turned family taverns and rotisseries into restaurants frequented by denizens of the first district, who pulled up in chauffeured cars and left bigger tips in a single evening than the proprietor's grandmother had earned in a month of operating the rotary iron.

Almost everyone who grew up in the Fourth came back eventually, at least to visit, to see if people still believed, to see if that belief still sprouted out of the concrete between rusty bikes and Vespas in back courtyards, out of the crevices between mattresses in red-light establishments, and out of the kitchen windowsill planters of rosemary. Some admitted they'd tried to forget or renounce the neighborhood, but none had ever succeeded.

The only piano bar in Kreis 4 was on Kanonengasse, and it seemed ashamed of the address. The single-story structure hid behind an apartment building from the fifties, illuminated in pink to mask its actual color. Faded lettering above the door read *Egger Coal Co.*

Pianos had always been a rarity in Kreis 4, and unless they had reason to, it wasn't like people went out looking for them. No one knew why the old coal depot had one—black, well-maintained, and in tune, *Ibach* stenciled in gold inside the lid—or who had donated it, but as far as superstition was concerned, this exotic artifact carried nearly the clout of a shooting star.

The man at the piano sat with his back to the crowd, an extended family of the disenchanted, who would sooner risk further disappointment than abandon the belief that the night still had something astonishing in store.

The pianist did not notice when around midnight, they all turned to stare at the stranger who walked in. He was focused on the satin curtain behind the piano. Beringed fingers with long, glittery nails parted the fabric to reveal five feet, eleven inches of pure sex appeal. Her hairstyle was plucked from the silver screen of the sixties; the black bowler hat, garter belt, and high heels from the seventies; her figure from the pages of the latest clothing catalogs. She had the best pair of legs in town and no need for shoulder pads. The smoke and metal in her voice and languid swing of her hips were known to beguile. At the end of the set, the crowd was howling within the first few measures as she closed with a little ditty about a gal named Tiger Lily.

The stranger had taken a seat off to the side at the very front, where the room was darkest and the view of the pianist's back unobstructed. His posture at the keyboard was strikingly erect, his bearing strikingly quiet. His arms moved only from the elbows down, while his shoulders remained still. Unusual for a bar pianist. He used the pedals sparingly, too, and neither hammered the keys nor sang along. The light gave his hair a golden glow, but it was clearly white.

After receiving a glass of the champagne the stranger had treated them to, the pianist stood, blinked into the half-light, and smiled vaguely. Large, slightly protruding incisors, his opened mouth unusually full and rosy for a man probably pushing seventy. As his lips parted, his high cheekbones were thrown into relief and his eyes turned into glittering slits. He continued to play solo, the tone more subdued, as though to allow guests the option of listening. No one was watching the stage now but the stranger. Tiger Lily emerged in jeans, a t-shirt, and sneakers, and sat down beside the stranger, beer bottle in hand. There were traces of makeup in his stubble, and the Monroe wig had left a groove across his forehead. New here?

The stranger gazed steadily at the pianist's back.

You bought me champagne. Tiger Lily's speaking voice was baritone. Everyone here knows that this is my poison after singing. He took a swig. The stranger leaned forward. Tiger Lily reached for the stranger's glass, held it up to the stage light, and set it back down. Water! Water at midnight! What, have you already dragged your way through all the finer establishments the Fourth has to offer? The stranger's silence was as smooth as his leather jacket. He's too good for a dive like this, isn't he? Tiger Lily teased. The stranger leaned farther forward. Lily leaned in too, his mouth now by the stranger's ear. My song? He composed it himself. He's all about Beethoven and stuff like that.

Tiger Lily gave up after the second bottle of beer. He sat there with his head tipped over the back of the chair and his long legs extended, when suddenly the stranger addressed him. What about Schumann?

What about what now?

Schumann. Can he play Schumann? "Träumerei," Please ask him to play "Träumerei" by Schumann.

Tiger Lily hoisted himself up, muttered something about Nazi film music, and shuffled toward the piano.

The pianist remained seated and asked Tiger Lily a question, probably double-checking. He must have been baffled by the request. He paused, motionless, as though he had to get his bearings, but did not turn around. It seemed he preferred not to know who had made the request, this request from another world.

Tiger Lily, wielding a broomstick and back in the stilettos from earlier, climbed on stage and pounded the wooden boards like a drum major until the room quieted. A long thirty seconds passed before the man at the piano began to play.

The stranger sat there with his eyes closed, not leaning on anything.

Notes rose hesitantly, like the memory of something distant, but never forgotten. It seemed the pianist wasn't so much playing as he was ruminating, straining to hear whatever it was his fingers would awaken. This was the wrong place for it, but the music was so quiet that everyone was listening.

No one noticed the stranger crying. After a few minutes, it was over. The resonance that followed seemed to forbid any other sound. No one applauded. It was only once the pianist rose and—moving gingerly, as though something had thrown off his balance—made his way toward where Lily was lounging, that the din resumed.

Lily stood and offered the pianist his seat, then ambled over to the regulars' table. On the wall behind it, colorful lightbulbs and plastic roses framed memorabilia honoring the bar's most notorious guests.

The stranger had slumped down in his chair. His upper lip trembled, but he was otherwise still.

It was you, the pianist said. You're the one who requested "Träumerei," aren't you?

The stranger turned his face toward him, a withdrawn, olive-hued face, as far as one could detect in the low lighting, evenly proportioned and ordinary.

Who are you? the stranger asked.

The pianist smiled again in the girlish way he had, winsome and warm. Are you asking who I am or what my name is?

The stranger did not reply.

My answer to question one is never satisfactory. I don't really know, no one does. I'm a lot of things and nothing at the same time. So, to answer number two: Kaufmann, Nico Kaufmann.

The barflies were all too focused on themselves to notice the quiet men sitting in the darkest corner of the room.

The stranger had lowered his head again and was speaking, although more to himself than in conversation. Was what happened with "Träumerei" really thirty years ago? Yes, it must have been. 1956.

So, when you were a teenager?

Fifteen, although I usually told people sixteen or seventeen. My God, there it is again. That's music for you. Crazy. Like it was yesterday. He fell silent. Madonna was singing "Like a Virgin." Kaufmann hummed along and waited. Tiger Lily set two glasses of red wine on the table. On the house, he said.

The stranger didn't thank him, didn't drink, simply gripped the stem of his glass and remained silent.

When Kaufmann asked the stranger what had brought him here, to this neighborhood, to this bar, at this hour, he didn't respond. Madonna was still singing "Like a Virgin."

Kaufmann repeated his question.

The stranger looked up. Are you Catholic?

Baptized, yes, Kaufmann said.

Deadly sins. My mother always spoke of seven deadly sins. Do you believe in any of that?

Can't say it's a topic I've ever discussed in a bar. Kaufmann took his first sip of red wine. So if that's what you want to talk about, but you evidently aren't drinking—he took another sip—then why go to a bar?

The stranger edged his chair in closer to Kaufmann. He'd been searching Zurich for a piano bar since that afternoon, he told him, looking for someone who could play Schumann's "Träumerei." What with the time spent abroad and living outside the city, he was now totally out of the loop. He had asked around widely whether anyone knew of a bar with a piano, be it a hotel bar or some trendy cocktail bar. The bar in Kreis 4 had been the eighth or ninth. The last one left.

But why, after thirty years, did you suddenly have to hear this one specific piece that's barely three minutes long, ideally even shorter?

I wanted to show my thanks.

Kaufmann faltered. To whom? The pianist who played it back then?

No, to the piece. I wanted to thank the piece. Without that piece, I'd've been . . . the stranger looked at his watch.

Dead for the last fourteen hours and thirty, maybe forty minutes.

Then he stood up.

I have to go, he said quietly and zipped up his jacket.

Kaufmann's right foot had fallen asleep, but he stood up too.

I'm coming with you, he said.

III

❦

THE BEDCLOTHES WERE TERRYCLOTH, patterned with gnomes. Wrinkle-free, Kaufmann said. My mother would have disowned me. Pure linen, monogrammed and starched—end of discussion. He stood at one end of the sofa, the stranger at the other; they were stretching a fitted sheet over the striped, velour Biedermeier cushions.

It hadn't been a long walk from the bar on Kanonengasse. They'd made their way through the clammy spring night in ten or twelve minutes. Kaufmann made it easy for the stranger. One could say he was recently widowed and welcomed the company, he explained, and the guest room was very comfortable. As they walked along, though, he realized there was something about the stranger's quick, dry yes in response that didn't fit.

He had escaped death, that much was clear, but of what nature? An assassination attempt? An accident, a robbery? Perhaps an incident on the operating table. Also hard to surmise what role "Träumerei" had played in all of it. The stranger seemed more than happy to spend the night, naturally at no cost, although between the shoes, leather jacket, and watch, his outfit was worth more than a week at the Baur au Lac.

Only once they'd changed the sheets on the big pillow, little pillow, and duvet did the stranger finally say thank you.

Would you like a nightcap? Maybe some port or Williamine?

No, thank you, said the stranger.

I could also offer you an aged Zuger kirsch.

The stranger shook his head.

From across the kids' sheets, Kaufmann studied him for the first time that night.

The stranger returned the gaze. It contained nothing threatening or devious, agitated or unstable.

There was something grim in it, though: his composure, after everything that had happened.

The stranger calmly said goodnight. Kaufmann obediently closed the guest room door behind him.

Nico Kaufmann's ability to sleep was the envy of his contemporaries; regardless of what he'd eaten, be it a working man's helping of fried potatoes or raclette, the moment he lay down, he was out until the next morning. It was now one thirty, though, and he lay there staring at the ceiling. He couldn't digest what the stranger had said. *Without that piece, I'd've been dead for the last fourteen hours and thirty, maybe forty minutes.* It was chilling. The stranger must have known that his host would be alarmed by the comment. Kaufmann's concern crackled with distrust. Perhaps his offer of the guest room was appealing because it was anonymous. The man was clearly untroubled by the impact his caginess had on his host's sleep patterns. Kaufmann's distrust gave way to flickers of rage. He was tempted to get up, knock next door, and shake the stranger awake, if he was already asleep.

Hospitality is holy, he heard his mother say with a smile after a guest had shattered one of her cherished gold-rimmed crystal goblets. Maybe not, then.

Then he heard something else. Not a full sentence this time, but the date the stranger had attached to his first encounter with "Träumerei": thirty years ago, 1956.

Kaufmann put on his robe and old silk slippers and crept down the hallway to the music room.

Rather than choose the comfortable armchair, he took a seat on the hard upholstered cherrywood sofa. His gaze fell upon the Steinway grand piano and the black-and-white photo displayed there in a silver frame. It was a large photo, the only one in the room. He knew the handwritten inscription above the autograph by heart.

For Nico. Practice makes perfect. One isn't born an artist, one must work to become an artist. This has been said time and again. To those who choose not to listen, however, best of luck on the path to brilliant mediocrity.

Thirty years ago, in 1956, Nico Kaufmann—professional conductor, professional pianist, professional composer—had already traveled that path. By age forty, he had long since arrived at its terminus.

In the Baur au Lac piano bar, he still managed to make an impression on hotel guests who didn't know much about classical music. Those who did either avoided the piano bar or indulged in the brilliant mediocrity as if it were a bubble bath. Kaufmann was happy with his pay, supplemented considerably by what guests left on the silver trays holding their champagne flutes.

Although he'd made plenty of friends (and attracted fans and lovers, at that) through the original compositions and arrangements he did for musical theater, or the dance numbers and couplets he wrote for the cabaret or private stage productions, the same could not be said for cash. He was treated with care at the Baur au Lac. He would make his appearance, this bar pianist in tails or a dinner jacket, lapels hand-stitched, carnation or gardenia boutonnière, his manners those of a grand seigneur, his hand-kissing perfectly timed, his small talk sophisticated, even in French, and above all, his levity, a quality wanting in most of his kind. Kaufmann knew them, of course, those working musicians just waiting for a free drink and the chance to lament the injustice of fate and outline the machinations that had hindered their path to stardom. Mozart came up a lot, often with a sigh. If only at age five, I'd . . .

Father Kaufmann—Willy Kaufmann, M.D., general practitioner and composer of infantry songs in his spare time—had dressed up his son Nico as Mozart when he was six and hosted public performances. He declared him a prodigy at age nine. When, at age twelve, Nico composed a Christmas carol and was accepted for piano and organ studies at conservatory the following year, this status was elevated to genius. Thus began a career destined to end in brilliant mediocrity. By the time Nico realized, it was already too late.

The man who had tried to save him from this outcome gazed silently from the silver picture frame. Pale, narrow face, protruding ears, prominent nose, shadowy bags under his dark, close-set eyes, his brown hair meticulously parted, his expression disdainful or disappointed or both.

The stranger entered without knocking. He'd pulled on his pants without socks, and his shirt was open. He paused. Kaufmann gestured toward the comfortable armchair.

The stranger followed Kaufmann's gaze, then turned the chair to face the piano and took a seat.

The photo was too large, the handwritten message too conspicuous, the man pictured too obviously unrelated to Kaufmann and too spectacularly melancholy, for one to avoid asking about it. Everyone always asked.

I wonder . . . the stranger began.

He stopped and kept his eyes on the piano.

Yes? Kaufmann said.

. . . if I might have turned out differently if I'd learned an instrument. It would never feel like the world was closing in, then, leaving no possibility to escape but death. Music, on the other hand, is ablaze with possibilities.

Was that what "Träumerei" recalled for him, the other,

better, more vibrant possibilities he'd seen at age fifteen? Kaufmann waited. Possibilities . . . June of 1956, early June. It was late and he was taking a break after churning out his standard bill at the Baur au Lac, when a man in a black suit came in carrying a violin case and sat down near the piano. He removed his cravat, draped it over the armrest, placed his order, and whispered something to the waiter.

Vodka? The clientele here typically treated Kaufmann to champagne—white or rosé—in exchange for a song. The man with the violin case, who appeared to be in his early to mid-fifties, smiled and raised his glass, presumably of vodka. Schumann's "Träumerei." Unusual request.

The other guests turned and stared as the violinist burst into raucous applause at the end of the three minutes.

Kaufmann didn't recognize the man until he was standing right in front of him.

He should have known. The festival at the Tonhalle concert hall. For weeks advertising pillars had been covered with posters bearing the names Nathan Milstein and Otto Klemperer.

You still play that better than Volodya. Really, you do, Milstein said. I heard him perform it just recently, as ever one of his favorite encores.

Kaufmann pictured his former teacher in the silver frame at home, disdainful or disappointed or both. It was all over, the possibilities squandered, the possibilities he'd had back then. The three minutes of this one little piece were all that remained.

* * *

The stranger couldn't have known what the mention of this date would unleash in his host. As it was, he seemed wrapped up in his own concerns.

Kaufmann tugged his handkerchief from his sleeve and wiped away the memory as he wiped his nose. Now was his chance.

What does "Träumerei" make you think of?

The stranger began to speak without turning, as though he were addressing the piano.

The job was good. No one asked for identification, and it made my parents proud to see their underage son work evenings and weekends at a place they would never have dared enter themselves. Emptying ashtrays, wiping down the little tables, lighting guests' cigarettes, distributing dishes of sweets, sweeping crumbs, making sure the Persian rugs weren't kicked up. My mother was certain God had gotten me that job in the Baur au Lac piano bar. Almost all of it was new to me at first. The soles of my shoes were unaccustomed to parquet and carpets, and my nose had never encountered the scents of perfume and Havana. The one thing that felt familiar was what the bar pianist played. I had grown up hearing other people's music through our open windows in Kreis 4. Nostalgic instrumental versions of hit *Schlager* tunes everyone knew by heart. Palms on the blue sea, brown girls in Cuba, the stars over Colombo, interspersed with film themes from *Casablanca* or *Some Like It Hot*.

They had only ever let me deliver room service a few times—there were special waiters for that. It was already quite late when they sent me with a bottle of rosé champagne and two glasses to room number whatever, second floor. When I knocked, a man's voice called out, Avanti. Did he know where I was from? Had he seen me, my olive skin and black hair, or was he Italian? He was lying on the bed. Naked. Naked and . . .

The stranger hesitated. . . . and beautiful.

I managed to set down the tray and close the door exactly as I'd been trained to, then hurtled down the two floors. I leaned against the wall outside the piano bar. Surely everyone could hear it: a frenzied pipe organ blaring within my organism, and inside my head, the collected priests of Zurich castigating my prostrate mother, as my little fan club of girls from the playground joined in her sobs. Then the maître d' came down the hall. And there I was, loitering at the height of the evening rush! I slipped inside before he reached me. It was scarily quiet in the bar. The guests were silent; the pianist was silent. Then he began to play a piece I'd never heard before. It was quiet, yet expansive, and came from somewhere deep inside.

Within minutes it was over. I couldn't help it—I had to approach him. What was that? I asked. Please, tell me what that was. He looked at me for a long time, clearly self-satisfied, sizing me up. You want to know what that was? He smiled. Just a little dream. He stroked my hair. "Träumerei," from the *Kinderszenen.*

* * *

Kaufmann shook his head and studied the stranger, as if he couldn't believe his ears. He shook his head again, harder. He rose in a daze, stepped over to the liquor cabinet, and poured himself a glass of the Zuger kirsch. You too?

The stranger turned his chair, shot back the kirsch, and eyed his host.

Is that why you wanted to know my stance on the seven deadly sins? Kaufmann asked. I was also born and raised in Kreis 4. Wiedikon, near the train station. Back then, in the twenties, it was a tidy middle-class area. Bougie, people in the Fourth would say now. My father was a doctor, which meant we had a maid, a cook, and a laundress. It meant antique furniture, a gramophone with the hand crank, an Ibach piano, mealtime prayers, a spot in the gallery at Saint Peter and Paul with our name on it, confession once a week, and faith in heavenly justice. Then there was the uncle who was severed from the family and called a sodomite behind closed doors. I was left with no other choice.

He paused, savoring the hunger he saw in the other man's eyes. He took a sip of kirsch and set down the glass.

I still believe in miracles.

He got up and went to bed.

IV

❦

FIRST LIBYA, which everyone was already used to. Libya and La Belle. Now everyone knew that pretty name, too, of a disco in Berlin where service members from the nearby U.S. Army base were known to dance their nights away. The threat of retaliation had been on the table since the early morning hours of April 5, when two American soldiers and a Turkish woman were slain in a bombing at La Belle. Twenty-five guests were injured but survived the bloodbath, while another two hundred fifty were happy to escape with nothing worse than burst eardrums. No one doubted Gaddafi's involvement in the attack.

Kaufmann hated the word *retaliation*. He dropped his croissant back on his plate to switch off the radio. Soccer and the weather were of no interest to him. The news bulletin was brief: Meilen on Lake Zurich. A Swiss diplomat in his mid-forties had been missing since yesterday. Police maintained suicide could not be ruled out. The man's fiancée, of Lausanne, disputed the claim.

Not five minutes later, the stranger appeared at the breakfast table. Piano music played on the radio.

That's not Schumann, is it? the stranger said, lowering himself onto the other chair.

Scriabin, Étude in C-sharp Minor. They're not playing it for the sake of playing Scriabin, though. It's because of Horowitz. He's performing at home again for the first time in sixty-one years. April 20, in Moscow. The Étude in C-sharp Minor is considered one of his bravura displays. *Bravura*— he would never use that word. This piece is far, far too dark for that.

Kaufmann would later say it was the stranger's interest in Horowitz that inspired the trip. The stranger would later say it was Kaufmann's instinct for what was right, his intuition that another person's story might help this chance acquaintance gain clarity about himself. In any case, there they sat, croissants not yet digested, in Kaufmann's old Peugeot, the stranger behind the wheel. Call me Robert, he'd said as Kaufmann lent him three shirts and three brand-new pairs of underwear. The rhythm of the windshield wipers made it easy for Kaufmann to tell his story.

It was in Basel, almost forty-nine years ago exactly, also in April, only the weather was nicer. You could call it a coincidence that we met. I'd call it . . . oh, never mind that. I was in my second season as a répétiteur at the municipal theater, the first chapter in my training as a conductor. They let me host colorful spectacles and direct Christmas tales I'd composed myself. The pinnacle was Mozart's *Schauspieldirektor*. Feel bad for me? Don't. It's still exciting when you're twenty-one. My father declared that, if not the next Liszt, his son might as well be the next Toscanini. He knew as well as I did that this was an evasion, or an excuse.

A Dutch painter, Bob Gésinus-Visser—really not bad, actually, influenced by the Nabis, Fauvists, and Neo-impressionists—anyway, he was just visiting Basel, and I met him through my friend Jörg, another painter . . . anyway, Bob heard I was a pianist and asked if I wanted to meet Horowitz.

Kaufmann eyed the man who wanted to be called Robert from the side. I don't know if there's anyone you . . .

Yes, Tina Turner.

I had seen Horowitz in concert two or three years earlier. Classical music isn't really your thing, is it? The crowds there applaud as if they'd be charged extra for clapping too much. But when Horowitz played, they were still on their feet after the third encore, and everyone's palms and faces were bright red as they were finally cleared out.

Bob had only recently met Horowitz, through the Bernoulli family. You're Swiss; that name hardly requires introduction. Everyone in Basel knew the house at 69 Holbeinstrasse, modest and trim from the outside, two squat stories, white-framed transom windows with shutters, but on the inside? Inside was Europe. The guests. Surely you understand. Peerless. Bernoulli—in this case, Christoph Bernoulli the such-and-such number—was an art dealer, interior designer, and musicologist from a family of musicians, while his wife, Alice, née Meisel, was a fashion illustrator and Polish Jew. As a Ukrainian Jew with Polish grandparents, Horowitz fit right in.

I was first vetted for Horowitz worthiness. I had to play for the Bernoullis after dinner, and my audition earned me a patronizing nod. Two days later . . .

He fell silent and became one with the windshield wipers, his breath matching their rhythm, but he did not speak. Several minutes passed before he said: This story would be better told on location.

By the time Robert parked on Steinengraben, he had heard the Rachmaninoff Piano Concerto No. 3 for the first time, as played by Horowitz; in fact, he'd had to hear it twice, under the domed roof of the car. One's amazement overshadowed the music the first time through, Kaufmann explained. Whereas this piece drove veteran musicians to madness, he played it at age seventeen, although at the time, he preferred performing Wagner's *Götterdämmerung* and Puccini's operatic oeuvre—all by heart, of course.

At his final exam in Kiev, he warmed up with a few pieces from Bach to Beethoven that had bested his peers, followed by Rachmaninoff's murderous Sonata No. 2 and the merciless Fantaisie in F Minor by Chopin, then finished it off with the Don Giovanni paraphrase by Liszt, which leaves you reeling just to hear. It was said to be the one and only time the jury had ever responded in the same manner as the audience at the Tonhalle fifteen years later.

* * *

The rain had subsided to a drizzle. The street was deserted and languishing. A few elegant baroque buildings cowered between the concrete of banks and insurance companies. Kaufmann stopped in front of a sixties-era monolith. It was somewhere around here. He hadn't been back since, and in those days it was a building from the twenties, a boardinghouse, nothing special. Horowitz avoided premier addresses—the Ritz in Paris, Les Trois Rois in Basel, the Baur au Lac in Zurich.

He kept his eyes on the façade as he spoke. Horowitz had rented an apartment on the second floor, just two bright rooms and a Steinway. He came to the door himself. He was a little shorter than me, and I figured at least fifteen years older, probably because of the deep wrinkles leading from his nostrils to the corners of his mouth. There was only twelve years' difference, though. The table was set for tea for two. No music, no radio, no phonograph.

Horowitz sat so he could watch my hands as I played. There was very little talking. Slower, he eventually said. That says crescendo, not accelerando. Playing louder doesn't mean faster. Or he'd say, Sing, sing with your fingers. He spoke with a Russian accent. My German is terrible, he apologized. My father spoke perfect German, what shame, do you say this?

I was about to close the lid when he stood and removed his coat. He didn't weigh much and had no biceps to speak of. His shirt was tight across his belly. It was a red shirt. He smelled of cigarettes and a cologne of violet, lavender, and coffee beans. He used two fingers to correct my hand position. His hands were narrow—small, really—pale and hairless, his fingers long and bony with blunt tips. What most struck me, though, were the muscles in his thumbs.

Kaufmann reached for Robert's hand. Do you see right here, where on you or me, there's just a slight bulge? On him, it was a rock-hard knob.

I awaited his assessment. He placed a hand on my shoulder. You're musical, he said, but you can't play piano.

Kaufmann opened an umbrella, handed it to Robert, and walked beside him, heading north.

Are there also certain lines in life you've heard and can never forget?

I just heard one, in fact, Robert said. I took the ferry across the lake yesterday, from Meilen to Horgen. There was an old man who doesn't seem to do anything but perch in the same spot and ride the ferry back and forth every day, and he said to me, Looks like the first time you've crossed to the other side.

And? Kaufmann asked. Was he right?

Was Horowitz right? Robert responded.

It was Darjeeling, Kaufmann continued, and he held the teapot high above the cups as he poured. I shouldn't, he said as he added a second spoonful of sugar to his cup, but I need it. Then he pulled up his pant legs. His calves were like twigs, despite the white bandages. Inflammation of the veins, he said. Not yet fully healed. They left me lying in bed for ten days following an appendectomy.

He repeated the part about those ten days a couple of times. He had always distrusted Parisian doctors and sought out the top surgeons, but got the same response every time: There's nothing wrong with your appendix, what do you want? They all refused to operate, until finally, one of them gave in. Those ten days turned into three months, purely because of the veins. He'd had to cancel his American tour. Then he said something vexing that I remember to this day. He said it very quietly. Good for the nerves, bad for the soul. Demons love the idle.

The two amblers stopped talking, and Kaufmann hummed a passage from the slow movement of Rachmaninoff's Third, until they reached the Bernoullianum, a spruce little palace of edification, even in the rain, which had picked up again. I couldn't have cared less about the architecture, the history of the old observatory, or the library and all that. What interested me was the park next door.

He veered to the right. The paths beneath the largely leafless trees were sodden; the bright green was dripping wet.

On my way home to the boardinghouse, I always encountered people here as hot to trot as I was.

Horowitz was in the dark about it. He had treated me to a pretty expensive dinner, complete with champagne, asparagus, poached Rhine salmon, and strawberries with vanilla ice cream. I figured he was trying to make up for the wound he'd inflicted, and besides, he didn't seem to know a soul in Basel, apart from the Bernoullis. After dinner he bought me one last drink at the bar three doors down. The alcohol made me sluggish. It came out of nowhere. I've booked a vacation in Lucerne, Horowitz said. Would you like a few lessons while I'm there?

Kaufmann paused, as though still startled by the offer.

It happened on the way back. I hadn't forgotten my manners—I wanted to walk him home—but my mind was befuddled. Why did Horowitz, who had never before had a student, want to spend his vacation working with a lousy pianist, who, at age twenty-one, was already too old to make it big? As for his personal life, I knew what everyone knew. Even Swiss women's magazines had covered that celebrity match: world's most famous pianist weds daughter of world's most famous conductor. Wanda Toscanini was a daughter by profession and didn't exactly appear alluring in photos, more like a sullen man dressed in haute couture. Still, it was his vacation. And then a student who promised to be nothing but trouble. What was he thinking?

Robert stopped walking because Kaufmann stopped walking.

Yes, this is the spot, somewhere around here, out of the wind. Horowitz wanted a smoke. He held the cigarette between his outstretched fingers, while I dug for a lighter. After I finally lit the cigarette, he took it out of his mouth, dropped it on the ground, and kissed me.

Robert slowly turned to face Kaufmann.

He was smiling.

V

Lake Lucerne slumbered that afternoon. The blue was still and deep, the woods around it dreaming. The tourists hadn't yet disturbed the scene.

An old Peugeot stood alone in the parking lot overlooking the lake, two men beside it.

I haven't been here in a long time, Kaufmann said into the distance. It's so beautiful.

But drowning is like suffocation, Robert's voice came from the side. Not a nice way to go.

I'd've expected you to know how to swim. Kaufmann's innocence was water-tight.

Robert gasped, then got behind the wheel and started the engine. How much did he know?

Sooner or later, Kaufmann would discover who was accompanying him on this trip into his past. Robert couldn't explain why the no-man's-land he'd occupied since yesterday meant so much to him, or why he felt the impulse to defend it as long as he could, although even as a child, he had wished for a cloak of invisibility like Siegfried, who saw without being seen. There was no better way to learn about other people and what they thought of you.

He had envied his psychoanalyst in recent years—no wedding band and no personal disclosures, whether sexual or political or ideological, his response to questions of this nature always a measured, Well, what do you think?

At the first red light they hit in Lucerne, Kaufmann rolled down his window and asked for directions to Furrengasse.

It was a better idea, they learned, to park in the garage and walk there.

Things were quiet on Furrengasse. No shops, no restaurants, no cafes, just a woman draped over her wheeled walker, who, approaching the men, stopped in her tracks at the sight of intruders.

This street was always dead, even back then, Kaufmann said, which suited my father just fine. He'd picked the room out specially for me. The other tenants' curiosity was part of the alarm system.

The smell of mortar and freshly poured concrete washed coolly over the men. Kaufmann stopped at a vacant lot, the neighboring buildings shored up, and sighed. They're destroying all traces of us. Maybe it's better that way. It was right here, a building from the seventeenth century or even older. The stairs creaked, the floorboards creaked, and the widowed lady of the house was a light sleeper. That was the other half of the alarm. Impossible to come home late undetected, especially with company. He grinned. It wasn't Horowitz my father distrusted. He aroused no suspicion. His first letter to me was addressed to my parents' home in Zurich, where I spent my weekends, because the boardinghouse marm in Basel read my mail. The letter was handwritten in German and about as erotic as an invoice. He included a list of pieces, with instructions to select a handful to prepare for my lessons in Lucerne. I still reread that list every so often: Bach, three pieces from the *Well-Tempered Clavier*, two in minor keys. Beethoven, 32 Variations in C Minor. Schumann, *Fantasiestücke* and Toccata. Chopin's Ballade No. 3 in A-flat Major and a total of four études from Opus 10 and Opus 25, all in minor keys. Next to several of the pieces, he'd written, Practice slowly!

My father told anyone who'd listen that his son was going to be the first student the world's greatest pianist—who had even surpassed Rubinstein—had ever taken on, and though it didn't come cheap, it was a luxury he was willing to allow himself.

There was just one person he distrusted: me. And with good reason. I wanted to be everyone's darling, regardless of education, pedigree, or gender, and did whatever it took, especially at night, to get my way.

Kaufmann gazed at the construction sign that depicted the planned development. It's a crying shame, he whispered and hurried on.

A breeze off the lake swept across Haldenstrasse. Number 57 could have used four house numbers. One for the front and three for the gables, each with its own name. *Carlton* to the left, *Hotel* in the center, *Tivoli* to the right. Tall evergreens and arborvitae framed the building.

It's supposedly not as posh inside as it was fifty years ago, Kaufmann said. It no longer attracts the well-heeled, who these days demand a jacuzzi in their room. A Steinway was all he needed.

The restaurant terrace was downstairs, on the first floor, by the big windows. It's still there, but no one will be sitting outside today, not in this weather. We lunched there daily, although unfortunately not alone. His wife had fled for London. There was nothing Wanda hated more than peace and quiet and a slowly convalescing husband, Horowitz said. But Sonia was there. I'll never forget how glorious the weather was in June of '37, because she called me *Monsieur blanc*, on account of the white suit I often wore. Sonia had smoldering eyes, hands soft as butter, an explosive laugh, and just one problem, which took the form of a forty-year-old governess. I did the math: Sonia would soon be three, meaning Horowitz must have gotten his marital duties over with during their honeymoon, following Christmas of 1933.

Kaufmann checked his watch. Five was as good a time as any for some rum with a little tea.

The lounge at the Carlton Tivoli resembled an opera star in forced retirement. It still made certain demands, and signs of its former glory remained. One was even tempted to applaud its impressive past, but there was no audience in attendance.

It seemed to do Robert good. He sank into the satin

upholstery, which had grown slick with grease over the years, and suggested they spend the night there.

Kaufmann took his time telling his story. Robert had time. For the first time since childhood, he had time. In fact, he'd been a child the last time he used as slow a mode of transportation as the train he'd lumbered along in yesterday, from the ferry dock in Horgen to Zurich. For decades, he had compulsively avoided any form of waiting, but now he luxuriated in it.

Kaufmann appreciated his patience.

Those first days of June in 1937 seemed to stretch out interminably before young Nico Kaufmann. He was expected to spend his mornings practicing; to that end, Father Kaufmann had arranged for him to use the piano at a nearby parish hall. Lessons were not held until the afternoon, as Horowitz insisted on a midday nap. Pre-lunch stroll—as a foursome—and following dinner, they would repair to a bar, albeit with a tail. I'm sure Wanda's paying her double for overtime, Horowitz scoffed.

The kiss in Basel had been a sign; Kaufmann had assumed Horowitz's invitation to continue as his piano student was a cover. Horowitz didn't touch him, though, at least no more than was standard and necessary between acquaintances. Not even a kiss on the cheek. Was Horowitz actually looking to test his pedagogical prowess on this young man? Instruction consisted of Kaufmann playing sections of the pieces he'd prepared while Horowitz sat in the same spot on the sofa, to the far left, and periodically raced to the bathroom, murmuring upon his return, I wouldn't wish gastric distress on anyone, even Rubinstein. He said little else. Never made eye contact when Kaufmann looked over. His own gaze wasn't suited to it, but instead turned inward and was too dark to distinguish iris from pupil. He didn't correct or even comment on hand position, fingerings, or interpretation. Whenever Kaufmann slipped, all that came was a tired, Slower. I told you to practice slowly.

Robert leaned forward. What were you thinking that whole time?

Kaufmann grimaced. He's like a cripple, I thought. Perhaps I should redouble my efforts to cheer him up. Defending my reputation as a raconteur was important to me. It seemed Horowitz had invited me to Lucerne as an antidote to his boredom. Many struggle with coming down from the rush of touring, so I served up whatever jokes, gossip, and anecdotes I could.

Were you successful? Robert asked.

I made up for it in other ways. There were plenty of prodigal sons and daughters running around who had as little patience for tranquility as Wanda.

You thought nothing more of it?

Sadly, no. Kaufmann's voice cracked. He cleared his throat to return to the story. The child and governess then left to visit Grandfather Toscanini at his vacation home on Lago Maggiore. Horowitz took pride in his daughter, by the way, and happily showed her off to everyone. Homemade, he would say. In truth, I'd always wanted to be a composer, but never managed. She's the one and only work I'll ever create.

At the sound of the tone signaling that hour's news, Robert strode over to the radio and turned it off. It didn't fit the mood, he said.

Champagne, asparagus, fish—presumably European perch—all followed by strawberries and vanilla ice cream? It seems you want to see me eat, Robert said.

It's my treat, Kaufmann said.

By the time dessert arrived, he was finally ready to continue. We lay beside each other in the king-size bed, student and teacher napping, with barely a stitch of clothing between the two of us. We lay there like that every afternoon.

Pretty harmless, he said, but enough for a scandal of unthinkable proportions, had anyone seen.

The clatter of dishes that floated into the room around four, as the terrace downstairs was set for tea, typically announced it was time to get up. Then came that one sleepy, sweltering afternoon. They awoke with a start at the sound of a violin in immediate proximity. It was coming from the suite's foyer.

Kaufmann stiffened at the very memory. I may have been callous, but in that moment, my heart stopped. Someone had gained access—a tabloid snoop, blackmailer, or paparazzo. I felt sick. My father! My family! His wife! The papers! My career!

And his, Robert said.

Yes, and his. Horowitz lay there quietly. He knows everything about me, he whispered, and has since we were seventeen.

Then I really started to listen. Whoever it was, was playing Paganini caprices—and how! I was embarrassed by my panic. Reporters, blackmailers, and paparazzi weren't exactly known for playing violin, let alone Paganini.

I met him over tea. Nathan Milstein. Same height as Horowitz, same age, nearly as famous, and also Russian. But at the same time, his exact opposite. Milstein was amiable; he loved women and champagne, ideally magnum in either case. He invited us out to a nightclub, a shadowy second-floor establishment on the banks of the Reuss. The kind of place with voluptuous ladies in fishnet stockings and false eyelashes, tabletop phones, decorative folding screens. Milstein was thinking less of himself than of Volodya. You'd be hard pressed to find a better cover for male lovers. My champagne buzz that night ended with me draped over a railing, vomiting into the Reuss. Horowitz just watched helplessly, while Milstein held onto me. No idea how they kept the stairs from creaking as they hauled me up to my room.

I had closed my eyes, my bed and the whole building a swaying ship. Then Horowitz kissed me.

Robert leaned forward again.

On the forehead, Kaufmann added.

You still sound disappointed, Robert commented.

Kaufmann's narrow eyes glittered. I was a junkie back then, but it wasn't dope or cigarettes or alcohol I was addicted to. Adoration was my drug. The more famous my admirer, the more powerful the high. Horowitz—well, you know. I didn't even realize what was going on with him. It was Milstein who tipped me off.

He was telling us about Paris, and it was downright electrifying, the way he went on. But Horowitz didn't react, didn't laugh, didn't chime in, didn't ask any questions. His expression was icy in the early summer heat. Have you heard my latest record? he asked Milstein. Some of it is good, but much of it is bad, very bad. What are they saying about me in Paris, about why I'm not performing? Is it true Toscanini's been saying I can throw in the towel if my next concert isn't a sensation?

Milstein simply asked in response, Are you practicing again, Volodya?

I . . . I'm trying, Horowitz said, studying his hands as though they were alien to him.

I caught Milstein as he was headed for the toilet. But why isn't he practicing, why isn't he playing, if it depresses him not to?

Turn things around and it all adds up. Nineteen thirty-four is when it started for Volodya. For a while, he could drown it out on the piano, on those murderous tours. All he talks about is his demons; he hoped they'd suffocate if he just kept moving.

But why, I asked, did it start in 1934?

When one aligns dates, it's often possible to discover connections, he said.

When Milstein left three days later, he took my hands in his, which to me looked like we were praying together. Be good to him, young man. No one before Volodya has ever played the way he does, and no one after him ever will. That tone! Sometimes I think tone means more to him than the music. He lived for that, and that alone. And for the money.

I aimed to please, and that included Milstein, so I begged Horowitz to let me listen to him practice. I actually begged him on my knees, which he liked. He hesitated, didn't respond. Late that night at the bar, he wanted to know where I had heard him play, and what.

At the Tonhalle in Zurich. You played the Tchaikovsky concerto.

And?

And I was in raptures.

It was awful, he interrupted me, because it wasn't Tchaikovsky I was playing, it was Horowitz. All sorts of things that weren't even on the page. Still, it worked. The more risks I took, the louder the applause when I survived them.

The crowd was looking to me for thrills, and that's what they got. But it was bad.

I tried to patch things up the next day at lunch. I was a born impostor. It wasn't his virtuosity that had done it for me, that night at the Tonhalle, I said. It was his tone. Never before had I heard someone play like that. That tone, that unbelievable tone!

He didn't respond. Then, finally, he said, Maybe in three days.

Following our midday nap three days later, he really did sit down at the Steinway, upright and earnest. Schumann's Fantasie in C Major. Hellish piece. Movement was confined to his elbows down, while his back and shoulders remained still. Hands flat, long fingers stretched out straight, fingertips practically curved upward. His pinkies curled, then sprang into action. Any piano teacher worth his salt would throw a fit at the sight of such hand positioning. Horowitz crashed down the octave runs as though taking a pleasant stroll. His staccato notes flickered off the page, and he sailed through the rapid changes in tempo and dynamics. But he kept stopping. He might play the same passage three, four, even ten times, changing the slightest nuance in pedaling or phrasing. Not once in my life had I practiced that way.

But that's not all. When Horowitz struck a key and immediately let off, the resonance unfolded in the space like magic, and the space unfolded into outer space. I was witnessing firsthand the birth of music through tone. I now understood what Milstein meant.

Our next nap was anything but sleepy. When he emerged from the bath, towel around his waist, Horowitz asked if I had a driver's license. He didn't have one, just a chauffeur who'd stayed behind in Paris with the Rolls. The hotel rented a car and . . .

Kaufmann checked the time. We should see about rooms.

By the time the Peugeot rolled out of the parking garage the next day, the morning drizzle had cleared. To the right of the exit, a newsstand owner tugged the plastic tarps off his racks.

Kaufmann scanned the headlines.

Robert looked straight ahead. He had already combed the papers, in the lobby before breakfast. Only two had touched upon the case, but hadn't included his name or photo, the details limited to *Unmarried lawyer from Meilen,* followed by a *45* in parentheses. Kaufmann noticed his searching look in the rearview mirror. You could easily pass for early forties.

What makes you say that?

Even approaching thirty-four, Horowitz didn't look much younger than you. Now I'll ask you to drive me to the same place I drove him that day. Hertenstein, a village in Weggis, right on the lake. My friend Sergei lives there, Horowitz said. He's been there for five years now. He built a house, a villa, and named it *Senar,* as in, *Se*rgei and *Na*talia *R*achmaninoff. Natalia is his cousin, and they've been married for ages. She's his life insurance. Sergei's nearly thirty years older than me, half a head taller, and those paws of his! When he covers my hand with his, mine vanishes. My friend Sergei's got me in the palm of his hand, all right. Horowitz abruptly fell silent. His silence vibrated. I heard Milstein's voice: My relationship with Sergei is uncomplicated. Sometimes he receives guests in striped pajamas, and given how bony he is, with that severe expression and close-shorn hair, he looks like a prisoner. It makes me laugh, and if it rubs him the wrong way, I just leave.

Rachmaninoff and Horowitz widely described themselves as friends, close friends, best friends. But it wasn't that simple between those two, Milstein informed me. Rachmaninoff would often tell people, Horowitz plays my third concerto better than I do, and if anyone failed to object, he'd storm out of the room. Horowitz had admitted to his friend Milstein that the first time he visited Rachmaninoff in New York, he was trembling so badly with fright that he could barely ring the doorbell. That was in his early twenties, but Horowitz was clearly still scared. He twitched, slid back and forth in his seat, and occasionally moaned, as though his stomach hurt.

Kaufmann instructed Robert to stop the car outside a white Bauhaus-style cube wedged into pillowy green private grounds.

This unapproachable building was a perfect reflection of the man of the house, I thought that day. And then . . . I stared at the front door, just as you are now. It opened onto Olympus. It was there that my god, Horowitz, met his god, Rachmaninoff, and now I, a twenty-one-year-old nobody *répétiteur*, would be joining them atop the mount. But why? Suddenly I realized why Horowitz was so nervous. His mother was dead, and although his father had visited him in Paris, it was probably the one time he'd ever be allowed to travel outside the Soviet Union. Horowitz was serious about me—about us. Rachmaninoff was his surrogate parent, and today was the day Horowitz planned to present his lover to the person most important to him. My trousers nearly burst with excitement.

Horowitz got out and approached the driver's side, where I was halfway out myself. Please pull the car back a little, he said. I reversed as he stood there gesturing. Farther, a bit farther. The villa was no longer in sight, which meant I was no longer in sight. Horowitz beelined for the house, as if he were pulled on a string. His body language forbade me from following. He certainly wouldn't be turning around. I threw open the door and tried to yell, but it came out like a weak bark. Back then, butcher shops still had those signs out front with the illustrated dog that read *No Dogs Beyond This Point*. I ran through my options. Honking, knocking, ringing, shouting. It all amounted to the same thing. Frau Rachmaninoff, or just one of their staff, would come to the door. Chauffeur? they'd ask. You're welcome to wait for him in the kitchen.

He wasn't going to introduce me. No, he wished to repudiate me. I was little more to him than an upscale hustler, only instead of taking his money, I gave him mine in return for instruction. The benefits I provided included musical ambition that served as a reliable cover, a reduced risk of syphilis, and a background above reproach. Son of a doctor, solidly bourgeois family that had by this point relocated to a lakefront manse. I waited, growing increasingly tired and empty.

More than two hours later, Horowitz opened the passenger-side door and took a seat beside me. Not a word of apology.

It was dark by the time we pulled up to the Carlton Tivoli. I parked under a pine tree, as far from the lights of the building as possible.

Neither of us moved a muscle.

Horowitz was waiting audibly for release.

I finally risked it.

Rachmaninoff despises homosexuals. Is that it?

Horowitz's hand was swift and strong. He pressed my face into his. This kiss was longer than the one in Basel. Much longer and much deeper.

VI

He couldn't help it. His right hand jerked toward his forehead and down to his chest, then lifted slightly to the left and to the right. He shook his hand roughly and trapped it in his pants pocket. A sidelong glance. Had Kaufmann noticed?

Robert hadn't entered a church in years, not even for his mother's funeral. If she wants to do right by me, she'll die while I'm far, far away and can't be reached, he had hoped. She did right by him.

Colorless glass windows, white floor tiles, white Baroque molding in the broad barrel vault. Everything light, yet oppressive. Two Benedictine monks in black cowls whispered beneath the pulpit; in the confessional, an old man was sobbing.

I know, you can never quite shake it, Kaufmann said, opening the door to leave. Pristine snow on the Alpine slopes, the sky overhead indifferent.

Kaufmann had been a boarding student here at Engelberg Abbey for just one year, when he was twelve. It was nice, he said, to be pronounced a boy genius by the music teacher, sing all the solos in choir, and get to sit by the organist and pull out the stops on Switzerland's largest pipe organ in short pants and socks studded with burdocks. He pretended to be asleep when one padre or another entered the dormitory at night and sat beside his bed.

Opportunists live longer, Kaufmann quipped, but his attempt to grin as he said it failed. Apparently others didn't get off so easy: refusal, defiance, and all other forms of insubordination were punished with bare-bottomed spankings, solitary confinement in the coal cellar, or having to kneel on rough-cut firewood. There was just one time Kaufmann mentioned to his parents how lucky it was that the padres loved him, really favored him, but otherwise left him alone, although it was clearly a struggle for them to do so. His father immediately brought him back home to Zurich.

And then that summer of 1937.

Kaufmann hummed as he said the word *summer*. Horowitz wanted to attend Mass in the Engelberg Abbey church, to catch a whiff of Catholicism, he said. Toscanini was rehearsing Verdi's *Requiem* in Salzburg at the time. Even his son-in-law knew that in his spare time, the Maestro was assessing the state of his virility at age seventy with the womenfolk of the Salzburg Festival. His wife and the god he prayed to averted their eyes.

Something recent—whether an event in the local village or Lucerne, or a smear story in *Der Scheinwerfer* newspaper—presumably inspired the priest to open that particular Sunday service in July of 1937 with a quote from the Book of Leviticus: *If a man also lies with a man, as he lies with a woman, both of them have committed an abomination: they shall surely be put to death.*

Horowitz's fingers cramped up and cracked, but he remained seated. Had he left the church with me, everyone would have turned and recognized us.

But why Engelberg, of all places?

The grand hotel there offered everything Wanda Horowitz hated, Kaufmann said. Peace and quiet, barely an hour outside Lucerne, but out of the way. And he loved that she hated it.

On July 3, 1937, Kaufmann received mail from Bagnoles-de-l'Orne in Normandy, where Horowitz was at a health spa, Wanda with him. *Write back and let me know if you can spend 4 to 6 weeks in Engelberg.* Instructions soon followed: *I arrive in Engelberg the afternoon of July 15 (between 3 and 6 o'clock). I'll be alone! Announce yourself on the hotel terrace immediately, so I know. À bientôt VH*

P.S. Unfortunately, I'll be traveling with my wife through Basel, but she'll then continue on to Italy.

Kaufmann watched Robert write *Widmer* on the guest registration form. Your hand doesn't like the *W* your last name begins with, he said.

They were led to the corner table, as requested, where he had sat forty-nine years earlier. Kaufmann felt the tablecloth, weighed the cutlery in his hand, flipped over the plate. Damask, silver, Swiss-made, same as back then. This was the table where Horowitz asked him where the local devil's haunt was.

He didn't know of any, at least none in the area. Why?

Angels and devils belonged together. He was both angel and devil himself, and always had been. Whereas other children sang to themselves while they played with blocks or did puzzles, the only place Volodya sang was at the piano. He would enchant his parents in the evening with spellbinding song, then destroy every last piece of porcelain in the house the next morning, swiping it off dressers, tables, and shelves with a stick. He had to bash it and smash it to keep from losing his mind.

Did he say why? Robert asked.

His parents' cook had shown him how a filter worked, and suddenly he understood what was wrong with him: he was missing the internal filter that served to protect normal brains. There was too much, far too much, getting into his brain, then as now, he said. It was absolute hell, but then again, it allowed him to hear sounds others couldn't begin to imagine. Sometimes he heard a silence that only God could know—the silence before the Creation.

Robert's plate of veal was getting cold, the creamy brown gravy developing a skin. Thou shalt not sin, his mother had cautioned whenever he failed to clean his plate. He mechanically shoved a piece of cold meat in his mouth and choked it down. He had shed that baggage, all those threats and towering promises, ages ago. On their second evening together, his fiancée had brought up having a church wedding. Never too late to return to the fold, and worth it in the long run. Haven't you heard of the light at the end of the tunnel that makes it all easier? Only those who pray and truly believe will see it when they die.

He hadn't even felt tempted to relapse after signing the paperwork at Ars M.

Suddenly they were back, though, angels and devils, hell-fire and sin, and all because of the story of a Jew who loved men, which was as deadly a sin for him as for a Christian or Muslim. The Book of Leviticus was in the Old Testament.

What did Horowitz believe in? Robert asked.

Kaufmann rescued him from the veal.

In music. And when things were good, he believed in himself. He would kiss his pinkies and say, They're divine, aren't they?

And what about God?

The greatest musician of all time, in his eyes.

There was a Steinway in his suite here in the summer of 1937 too. Horowitz played for his student, often selecting pieces by composers whose names Kaufmann was hearing for the first time, such as Medtner or Kabalevsky. You can learn by listening, he said, if you listen well. It's best you learn how to listen first.

Kaufmann fell silent and stared blankly, as though listening for a fading sound, like that of a band marching into the distance.

Listening. Listening. I was consumed by looking.

When he sat at the piano with the scent of hay floating through the open windows and the afternoon light hitting the red blinds, that leaden gloom disappeared from his face.

The what? Robert asked. What disappeared?

The leaden gloom.

Sometimes they were surprised at lunch, other times in the early evening: Horowitz would be called to the phone. He would get up nervously and rush out. If he returned, he'd be sweating from every pore, gasping for breath. He wiped his forehead with a napkin or the tablecloth, tore off his bowtie, and feverishly unbuttoned his collar. And there it was again, that leaden . . .

Kaufmann pulled out his wallet and produced a photo, a snapshot, of Horowitz looking happy. He covered the eyes. Look at his laugh. It's the explosive laugh of a child.

Then he covered the mouth. But now look. Nothing there but gloom.

It had taken no more than a pleasant kiss, or maybe two or three—the waitresses tasted like caramel—for Kaufmann to discover who was calling, or demanding to be called back, every day. It was Madame Horowitz.

He never called her Wanda. It was always *my wife*, or occasionally *Madame*. Her father was never Arturo, and only rarely *my father-in-law*. He was usually *Toscanini* or *the Maestro*.

Wanda. Kaufmann often repeated the name to himself, to conjure up a sense of the woman. Wanda. What a dramatic, operatic name, as if her surname weren't enough. He'd had a classmate in grade school named Attila. Whenever Attila said his own name, people would kick him in the shins. For the first time, it dawned on Kaufmann what a burden being Toscanini's daughter must be.

He pointed his fork at a sideboard against the opposite wall. There used to be a radio right there.

On July 30, 1937, Horowitz had two chairs set up directly in front of the radio. Toscanini was conducting a Mozart opera for the first time ever at the Salzburg Festival. The first act was already over. Horowitz cursed the bourgeois early-bird diners and *Schlager* music fans, who were to blame for that. But there he sat, his palms pressed together between his knees.

Tamino sang, *Pamina mein! O welch ein Glück!* My Pamina! Oh, what happiness!

In a second you'll hear the maestro, Horowitz whispered. He doesn't speak German, but he memorized the entire libretto. Everyone's afraid of him—the singers, the orchestra, his wife, his children. He's awful. Merciless.

And there it was, Toscanini's thin voice singing along with Tamino from the pit. *Hier sind die Schreckenspforten, die Not und Tod mir dräun.* These are the fearful gates, which threaten me with danger and death. Then Toscanini joined Pamina. *Ich werde aller Orten an deiner Seite sein.* I would be everywhere at your side.

Horowitz was shaking. His hands were shaking between his knees, and his knees were shaking. The maître d' placed a plaid throw on his lap, set down a cup of hot chamomile tea beside him, and turned off the radio.

Horowitz remained seated and the shaking subsided. She'll protect me. She can, and she will. Toscanini's daughter. People fear her too.

Kaufmann closed his eyes.

He didn't want to be alone that night. The curtains were drawn, the bed turned down. I knew that outside, the night was warm and bright, the air saturated with the scent of Alpine meadows, honey, and evergreens. I thought I might suffocate. Horowitz had withdrawn to the bath. I shoved the velvet aside. The blinds were down, the windows latched. I yanked up the blinds and threw open the windows to listen and smell and take in the moonlit night, but he started screaming. You idiot! You ruin my sleep, you ruin me. Idiot!

Two room attendants were summoned. Horowitz didn't calm down until they had sealed off every last crack in the shutters and the curtains and wedged a draft stopper at the base of the blinds.

On the left nightstand was a German newspaper article that had been folded into a rectangle the size of a letter. *Homosexuals are a dangerous manifestation of degeneracy. Heinrich Himmler has announced a campaign to combat this threat to the master race.* There was a note scribbled in the margins in green ink: *Apparently being Jewish isn't enough for them, he says about people like us. He hates the fact he can't have gay Jews liquidated twice over. Volodya, come here before it's too late. Cesco.*

I knew who Cesco was, thanks to Alice and Christoph Bernoulli in Basel. I'd been trying to learn more about Horowitz through them.

Cesco—Francesco von Mendelssohn, that is—was utterly flawless to behold, whether in red leather, a yellow evening gown, or nothing but his body hair. It was something his hosts at 69 Holbeinstrasse knew as well as his lovers, considering he never closed the door, be it to the toilet or his bedroom. The prim façade of 69 Holbeinstrasse may have concealed Europe behind it, but that wasn't all. It was also one of the continent's most sophisticated gay hubs. Gustaf Gründgens, Magnus Hirschfeld, Harald Kreutzberg, Ramon Novarro, Klaus Mann, Jean Cocteau, Horowitz. And Francesco, descendent of Moses Mendelssohn, heir to millions and a brilliant cellist. Cesco had once tried to steal Horowitz's so-called secretary Jonny, whom he'd been living and traveling with for six years at the time. Horowitz had a fit when Cesco made a pass— Jonny was a good boy, he said, and this attempt to corrupt him was downright disgusting. Horowitz and Cesco made up eventually. Since his marriage to Wanda, every spurned lover seeking revenge had become a powder keg.

There was nothing I wouldn't endure in my effort to make Horowitz need me. I let everything go, like when he blubbered over a broken fingernail or fussed about the poached trout to the point where even I couldn't stand the sight of it. Or when he made me play through an entire étude, only to say, I could tell from the very first measure that wasn't going anywhere.

He was very careful, constantly on guard, and not just when we dined together on the terrace or went for walks, which Rachmaninoff had prescribed to combat his depression. Horowitz knew that when I was in Zurich, I lived with my parents on Seefeld Quai, meaning my mail passed through their hands too, and although he was embarrassed by his mistakes, he wrote almost exclusively in German, something he never explained to me. It was his idea for us to devise a code for our letters. *Playing Chopin* referred to heterosexual intercourse, whereas *playing Brahms* meant homosexual intercourse, and *playing Jonny*... well, I'm sure you can imagine. His coming up with the expression *little animal* seemed a bit risky, because honestly, who wouldn't see through that? But he adored the little animal and giggled childishly about anything related to either his or mine. I considered it a point in my favor whenever he was in a good mood, but whenever his melancholy returned, I couldn't help but feel somehow responsible.

Whenever he received a telephone call, for instance, and he returned, sweating, and yanked off his bowtie, and...

Pardon me, gentlemen.

A man clad in the armor of corporate knighthood—three-piece suit, dive watch, distinctive tie—approached the table, pressed his right hand against his chest, where the vest bulged out, and nodded slightly in Robert's direction.

I may be mistaken, but are you Herr Donati? All I've seen is a photo of you. That's my fiancé, my sister said, and...

What was your name? Robert asked.

The corporate knight stated his name, and Robert began tugging at his collar. They all watched the mother-of-pearl button skitter across the table and drop onto the parquet floor, then roll under the sideboard that had once had a radio on top.

Forward flight, Kaufmann called it.

Among rows of files, the only open wall space was dominated by a large crucifix, blanched and bloody, and the clock above it. Local visitors to the Engelberg police station did not appear to notice. Donati stood with Kaufmann at the front desk, his Adam's apple bobbing.

What's the opposite of a missing person report? he had asked.

Found item? one of the officers tried, but his colleague shot it down. For a minute or two, the ticking of the clock was the only sound in the room. Donati decided to skip any flourish and stick to simple prose. The officers' faces were lit up like Christmas trees—this station didn't see much excitement.

Reason for the hasty departure from your house in Meilen, Dr. Donati?

Personal.

Reason for disappearing?

Personal.

Purpose of your current travels?

Personal.

The clerk recorded the word *personal* three times, not bothering with follow-up questions, save one: whether his fiancée should be informed.

I don't think that's necessary at this point.

As Donati and Kaufmann exited the building, they were blinded by the flash of a camera. Squealing tires, roaring engine. They failed to catch the make or plate number.

Their thoughts remained inside the building, though they now stood outside it.

Both men breathed audibly, as though it might help retrieve those thoughts.

Horowitz loved this air. With the mountains so close, it's totally untainted. Air is like music, he said. It frees you from constraints, and it cannot lie.

Donati immediately responded. Is that verbatim? He said constraints?

I believe so.

Kaufmann withheld the fact that the part about lying had troubled him most. He had been an acrobat in those days, on the tightrope of—lies? No, of diplomatic solutions, peaceable evasions, and sleights of hand that made life easier for everyone, himself included. If it was true, though, that music couldn't lie—unlike language or pictures—then it wouldn't abide such deceptions as these. Perhaps this emotional truth was precisely what his piano playing lacked. Kaufmann, however, would not come to this realization until much, much later. At the time, he simply wondered if

Horowitz had mentioned lying because his lover's dalliances actually hadn't escaped him.

Do people know you? Donati asked.

Kaufmann stared at him. What do you mean . . . do people know me?

Are you known for being active in certain circles?

Active? Kaufmann blinked at him. Keep going, you're making me feel important.

Donati was not amused.

. . . Certain circles? Yes, there are two. The first is Kreis 4, as you well know. Then there's the *Kreis*, the Circle, Switzerland's oldest gay organization and magazine by the same name.

Their thoughts turned inward as both silently ran through the possibilities.

Are you worried about what people might think? As he spoke, Kaufmann looked down the street, where nothing littered the pavement. There were no bikes leaned against building walls, no kids dripping their ice cream, no one shuffling their feet, no mess left behind by a dog. There was nothing here that might flake, crumble, or stink.

Donati did not respond.

Inescapable, he finally whispered. This street is monstrous.

He wanted to return to Zurich.

Kaufmann was proud of his reputation as a good travel companion, a smiling passenger-seat Buddha, hands resting on his belly. When he confessed to being a lousy driver, at that, there was no stemming the sympathies showered upon him. This, however, was unpleasant. Donati passed in blind curves and slowed down as he did so. He braked before speedbumps, kept his eyes on the rearview mirror, and accelerated at the sight of a speed limit. He grabbed at his throat and opened the window; there was a terrible draft. He rolled the window back up and asked Kaufmann to open his.

It's the woman making you nervous, isn't it? Kaufmann finally ventured. His wife—that's right, that's where we left off. During that four or five-week period with Horowitz, I was determined to find out why Wanda made her husband sweat the way she did. A week and a half passed before I recalled what Milstein had said: When one aligns dates, it's often possible to discover connections. Finally it hit me. I don't know how I could've missed it: Horowitz had been depressed since 1934, and 1934 was his first year of marriage.

I could sense he was relaxed, lying beside me, puffing evenly on a cigarette, exhaling toward the ceiling, and I felt okay asking why he had married Wanda. His response was so strangled, I had to strain to hear him.

When he met her at a party in New York in the spring of 1933, after his first joint performance with Toscanini, he felt there was nowhere he belonged. He had parted ways with his Russian manager and quit the trio with his friends Milstein and Piatigorsky in favor of a solo career. Returning to the Soviet Union was unthinkable, as he'd heard even musicians had fallen prey to the gulag. Berlin, where he had always felt free, loved, and understood, was now poisoned soil for Jews. Jonny, his German secretary, had announced his intention to marry, to avoid any trouble.

Every living room in Russia has an icon in it, Horowitz suddenly stated. It's always hung in a corner, up higher and different from the other pictures. The entire room, in fact, exists solely for the icon. Home is where the icon is. If an Orthodox Christian loses his house, if he's sent to prison or forced to emigrate, he'll slip a small icon in with his things. That way, he's always got home in his pocket. We don't have anything like that. But to me, Toscanini is an icon, and his daughter is part of it.

Over the next few days, all Horowitz wanted to hear me play was Chopin's Étude in C-sharp Minor, Opus 25, No. 7. It's the only slow one, not much for dazzling the crowd. It opens with a monophonic recitative highly reminiscent of the baritone line from the *Ode to Joy*, in Beethoven's Ninth. The Beethoven piano sonatas, Horowitz concluded, were written for bad pianists. The single great work of Beethoven's to reach his fingers around that time, though he never hesitated to alter his stance entirely, was Liszt's transcription of the symphonies. In its original form, Horowitz thought the Ninth reckless in asking singers to unleash full pathos at the tops of their voices after interminable waiting. Of all pieces, then, why this étude?

You need an audition piece, he explained. Audition? What for and for whom? I wasn't planning a performance, and I'd already taken my exams. Besides, playing Brahms felt far more important. But Horowitz was adamant. *Innig*, he repeated over and over as he listened. Earnest. He used German words you rarely heard. You must play this earnestly. His nostrils flared as he said it, like when he played an especially difficult passage.

He was leaving for Salzburg, for the final days of the festival and *Fidelio* under the baton of Toscanini, who'd apparently taken Leonore as a lover.

Beethoven's opera fell on deaf ears, as far as Horowitz was concerned. It wasn't a proper opera—a dramaturgical nightmare, more like—and besides, he found Salzburg unnerving, what with local dignitaries turning out in traditional garb. Still, he had to make an appearance. The whole clan, Wanda's sister and brother-in-law included, expected him, and they'd all be sharing private quarters outside the city. He got in the taxi as though headed for his own funeral. I held the door. Wait just a minute, wait. He scribbled *Horowitz c/o Toscanini, Villa Baillou, Liefering bei Salzburg* on light-blue hotel notepaper. Write to me. Write to me at least twice a week, and respond to my letters immediately. I'll be waiting for them. Practice the étude. *Très melodique* and serious, do you hear me? Serious!

Donati repeated the word under his breath, as though trying to taste what was off about it. He didn't speak again until just outside Zurich.

You're a clever man, Kaufmann finally said. *Serious* was not a word that applied to me. Nor was *earnest*.

* * *

Things were slow in the bar at the Hotel Bellerive that evening. Still early, the bartender explained, polishing the art deco fixtures with a soft cloth. Fine by him, Kaufmann said. He also wouldn't say no if his companion offered to buy him a drink. What with a lakefront villa in Meilen, a glass of champagne shouldn't present too great a hardship.

He received a hint in October of 1937 to help solve the riddle behind the audition piece. He would be in Zurich from October 20 to November 10, Horowitz wrote, and Nico should book him a suite—not at the Bellerive, his standard choice, luxurious but second-tier, but at the Baur au Lac. My wife will *only stay at this hotel*. Kaufmann did everything right, practiced as he was at walking the high wire of—lies.

Unfortunately, Madame's desired accommodations were booked solid during the period in question. Might he suggest the Bellerive?

It was a beautiful corner room two floors up. Horowitz was alone the first few days. Then there she was, sitting beside him on the cherrywood sofa at the Kaufmann family residence at 17 Seefeld Quai. Her eyes were deep-set and cobalt blue, her eyebrows straight, bushy, and black; the crease between them betrayed the wrath within. Toscanini's daughter to a T. She wore white makeup and thick, garish red lipstick.

Could he play something for his wife? Horowitz asked his student. She spoke French, even with him, an angular, almost jagged French. Not a word of German.

Kaufmann understood now why Horowitz wrote him in German.

I particularly enjoy the Chopin étude that opens like the baritone recitative from Beethoven's Ninth, she said. As you know, my father and Beethoven, it's like . . .

Oh, I know, Madame, said Kaufmann. I know. He could tell Horowitz was sweating from every pore, fiddling with his collar. He felt hot too. This was about proving his student status—it was possible Wanda suspected something. Kaufmann could hear Milstein in his head. We were all surprised when Horowitz broke it to us: I'm engaged to Toscanini's daughter. He was surprised himself. What do I even want from her? he asked us. Women are unnecessary baggage. My fiancée can't do a thing but tell me whether I played something well or poorly.

That she could.

Kaufmann finished playing. Silence.

No applause from his father, no applause from his mother or teacher. He sat glued to the piano bench, and the silence stiffened like his back. Wanda Horowitz then clapped her hands—hard and dry, as though wearing gloves—four or five times.

Kaufmann stood, watched Horowitz place his sodden handkerchief on the tea table, and tried to catch his eye. Horowitz was staring at his wife's teacup. Her red lipstick glowed against the white porcelain rim.

What was it like? Donati asked. Do you remember his expression?

Disgusted, Kaufmann said.

Donati ordered a second round. He needed another half glass.

In my classified ad, I specified: Natural look and slender preferred. When we first met, she held out both hands. Chubby hands with long, red fake fingernails.

Thomas Mann hated that too. Called them red claws.

You knew him? Personally, I mean?

Kaufmann nodded.

Donati threw back the rest of his champagne with his eyes closed and his left hand gripping the edge of his seat.

Kaufmann watched him. By the way, the Circle hasn't existed in nineteen years. Same goes for the magazine.

Donati stifled a yawn, leaned back, stretched out his legs, and crossed his arms.

Something tells me you're relieved to hear it, Kaufmann said. Too bad, he added quietly.

VII

❦

KAUFMANN WATCHED the key repeatedly miss the lock as Donati endeavored to open his front door. Then came a dry rustle. Donati waded through the mail on the floor without glancing down, let alone reaching for it. The entryway smelled of nothing. It smelled so strongly of nothing—no hint of human or animal presence, wood, food, or even potting soil, furniture polish, cleaning products, or stale air—that Kaufmann distrusted his nose. By the time they reached the room with panoramic windows, which must have been the living room, Kaufmann's gaze had not encountered a single thing on which it cared to linger.

Donati collapsed into a white leather armchair and gestured toward the white leather armchair opposite. The grandfather clock set the rhythm for their silence. Donati had insisted on showing Kaufmann his house. It had sounded to Kaufmann like he was finally ready to reveal who he was. Perhaps he assumed that the house said it all, home to no one and flanked by a scrubby, flowerless garden even now in mid-April. Kaufmann waited. Donati appeared to be waiting as well, but what for? A comment on the architecture or location? Or for Kaufmann to ask what he'd run away from or if anyone had ever lived here with him?

There was an oblong, black-lacquered set of drawers against the wall beside Donati, chest-height and the size of a dining room table. One shallow drawer sat atop the other, each no deeper than a handbreadth.

What is that—what's in those drawers? Kaufmann's voice echoed.

My butterfly collection. Would you like to see?

I'd rather not. I used to be one, Kaufmann said.

A butterfly collector?

No, a butterfly. Could you open a window, please?

Something was in bloom, after all, perhaps in the wild or a neighbor's garden. Kaufmann drank in the air like someone returning home. Then he asked why Donati collected butterflies.

No, not for scientific purposes. I love them, especially the ones that shimmer and glow. I'm obsessed. I've hunted them since I was young, but their fluttering disturbs me, nearly drives me insane. Only once I've pinned their bodies do I feel at peace.

Kaufmann studied him as he spoke. Donati's face appeared longer and narrower, his nose bigger and skin paler, and suddenly he noticed the bluish bags under his dark eyes. He saw Horowitz sitting there. You'd've gotten along well, he said.

Who? Donati asked.

You and Horowitz.

On the shelves to Donati's other side, beneath brightly colored, almost identically shaped vases and books arranged by size, he spotted a record player and behind it, the sleeve. Donati followed his gaze.

Is that the record you last listened to? Kaufmann asked.

Donati did not respond.

Kaufmann was at a loss, and he suddenly sensed how exhausting it was. The conversation was going nowhere, like a car stuck in the mud. With every second that passed in silence, the ruts grew deeper.

The noise resounded, terribly loud and terribly close. They both jumped. Then came another crash. Neither man showed his surprise; they both now listened for the sound. By the third time, shock no longer impeded identification. Something hard was hitting the aluminum-clad front door.

I'm not expecting anyone, said Donati.

Kaufmann's quiet *You should probably answer the door* fell on deaf ears.

Kaufmann went instead. At the door was a woman holding two golf clubs. She wore a weatherproof jacket, and her fine, pale blond hair framed a marzipan oval with a beautiful vermilion mouth. Nothing in her expression changed as she found herself face-to-face with a stranger.

I figured as much, she said. The guy from the photo. She pushed past Kaufmann and stormed into the living room. She sent one club clattering across the marble floor and gripped the other in a red-gloved hand.

You could have cheated on me with a woman, she said. Spared me my dignity. She lifted the golf club, angled it into the right corner of the nearest cubby, and swept all of the books there onto the floor.

Kaufmann didn't dare restrain her. His *Stopstopstop!* foundered laughably in the room. Donati's slack posture betrayed that he was prepared to let it happen.

She cleared off one shelf after the other. The white floor was strewn with colorful kaleidoscopic shards of broken Venini vases. She was controlled and to the point; she didn't scream or even groan, but the strain in her neck and sweat on her forehead and nose betrayed the effort it took.

Donati sat there, frozen in the ice of his leather armchair.

The entire wall unit was gutted. She approached the record player, lowered the golf club, and paused. Donati did not turn his head. She reached for the sleeve and said, You even marked it, three minutes, one second. Then she opened the lid of the player and dropped the needle. The opening chords of "Träumerei" rose over the destruction. To Kaufmann, there was more life in this battlefield of busted glass and splayed glossy books than what had been there before.

Kaufmann heard it before he saw it. Donati was crying, the tears emerging from his dry face like the first rain following a drought.

Donati's fiancée regarded him as would a farmer who had prayed for rain, only to be disappointed by the pitiful drizzle that finally fell. She checked her watch. Two quick steps, the needle scraped across the record, and the music died.

The fiancée dropped the record on the floor in front of a rigidly tearful Donati, then stomped on it repeatedly with her sharp heel. She gathered the golf clubs, stood up tall, proud, and free, and left. The door closed quietly behind her.

Donati's tears trickled away. His eyes seemed to plead, Speak, tell me a story, just say something.

Kaufmann searched for the right response.

Powerful performance.

Out of the question.

How dare she suggest that we . . .

That was no good, and besides, she could easily think that, what with the picture and her brother at the hotel.

What she said is nonsense, of course, that she'd be better off if you'd cheated with a woman. That nonsense was not uncommon, though, for a woman to think her husband had turned gay because the sex with her was bad. Inappropriate, totally inappropriate, to say that, though. Not least because Donati still seemed so unformed.

Dignity—strange word choice, Kaufmann said. The first my parents ever spoke of dignity was as death approached.

Donati shot out of his chair and over to the panoramic window.

He spoke into the window, his back to Kaufmann, shoulders tensed, hands in his pockets. . . . *for all guilt is avenged on earth.*

My foot! thought Kaufmann. Those words were disproven by the very poet who wrote them. Goethe had deserted his bosom friend Lenz and didn't bat an eyelash when his old pal perished namelessly in a Moscow gutter and his body found use as a cadaver; nevertheless, Goethe's reputation as a benefactor remained unsullied. Goethe let his own wife die in abject solitude a few rooms away, wracked and wailing with pain. He, on the other hand, died comfortably. It would set a few things straight to tell that story, but to speak of death right here and right now, in a house that may never have lived, it felt so dead? No. Kaufmann rummaged through his memories in search of a story, an anecdote, some lived experience that might contain a bit of advice. His stories seemed to do Donati good. Kaufmann himself had always liked the fairytales his grandmother, mother, or father told, of animals that helped humans, simply because they had listened to them; of the cowards, the courageous, and the cocksure who used cunning to unleash untold violence; of fools who recognized that the big questions were actually very simple; and of aged sages who guided the errant back to love. It would be best to continue telling him about Horowitz.

Up next was Paris, where Horowitz had established a home of sorts in the winter of 1937 to 1938, and where he'd invited his student to continue private studies with him through the end of March. He and Wanda were at the Hotel San Régis, two rooms, genuine rococo furnishings, Persian rugs, Steinway in the parlor, and marble bath, while Kaufmann was installed in the guestroom at the home of family friends. The apartment was well-situated and his hosts had no desire for interaction, much to his relief. Paris was a meadow in full bloom, where the butterflies simply fluttered away over the starving bellies of the unemployed, the sooty sweat of demonstrators, and the panic of those who had escaped Hitler's slaughtermen. Kaufmann could still clearly recall posing nude for photographs in the studio, a blond Greek god; gazing reverently upon Jean Marais's magnificent genitalia on display in the theater green room; and feeling the skilled hands of the Algerian masseur pampering him in the hammam at Les Bains Russes. None of that was appropriate, though, to what had just happened here.

The room was still charged with an explosive combination of rage and fear, helplessness and belligerence. A single spark, and the whole thing would blow.

. . . *for all guilt is avenged on earth*, Kaufmann repeated softly. So that means you believe in justice? Even earthly justice?

He should have bitten his lip, something he never did, for the sake of his lips; Donati was a lawyer, a top lawyer.

He stood like a pillar against the grayish blue of the lake and sky.

Clouds crawled past. The light was gentle, the air calm.

An expansive view makes you feel expansive yourself. At least that's what I thought, Donati said.

But things kept closing in, Kaufmann responded.

Donati spun around. Where did you . . . What did you just say?

I'm talking about Horowitz in Paris. He had to watch through the bars of the cage he shared with Wanda, as I, the butterfly, flew from flower to flower. Horowitz suffered.

But you didn't care?

Donati's tone was suddenly animated.

This made Kaufmann as happy as he felt upon spotting the first flower breaking through the snow in February. Without raising his voice he said, Horowitz orchestrated the whole thing. I'd expected Wanda to leave at some point, but she never did, other than the occasional shopping spree for jewelry or couture. I arrived in Paris with a clear image of the enemy tucked in my luggage: she was the reason for his depression, and his depression was the reason for his stage fright; therefore, Horowitz had to leave her. Evidently, however, the two were pursuing the same plan, in which I served as an in-house paramour whose presence Wanda tolerated. I was supposed to get Horowitz back in running order and performing on stage. Wanda had married him because he, like her father, was the best of the best in his field. If he failed to demonstrate that in public, then her husband was of no use to her.

It seemed Paris was intended to be a test run of sorts. Once she gave her nod of approval, he was allowed certain discreet freedoms. The arrangement irked Horowitz. He was irritable in Wanda's presence, extremely irritable. He stewed in silence, then exploded out of nowhere. If there was one thing I understood, it was this: her insistence that he suppress his homosexuality was like a boulder lodged inside the crater of a volcano. There was no telling when it might erupt.

Milstein once told me that Volodya had always loved wearing custom-tailored pink shirts. He hadn't worn a single one since his engagement to Wanda. But, Milstein said, that doesn't mean he threw them away.

Donati leapt toward Kaufmann, pulled him from the chair and down a corridor to a narrow room with an entire wall of mirrored wardrobes, and slid one of the doors open: hanging there back to chest, back to chest, was a wall of pink shirts five feet wide. Donati swayed, leaned against the wall, and closed his eyes. Go on, he groaned. Go on.

Here? Kaufmann asked. Really, here?

Donati paused, his eyes still closed.

What about the other room? Kaufmann asked. Who's going to clean that up?

Donati did not move. Kind of you to ask, but it will be taken care of. Please continue.

On New Year's Eve we dined at Le Boeuf sur le Toit, the eatery of the Parisian elite, and Wanda wore a floor-length Elsa Schiaparelli cape over her dress with some sort of gold embroidery. Horowitz and I caught each other's eye shortly before midnight. Two or three church bells had started ringing early, and we rose, bubbly in hand. Now we could see what was sewn on Wanda's cape in gold sequins: a dragon. While the others drank a toast to the new year, he and I clutched our glasses and stared at that dragon.

Horowitz was superstitious. Dragons guard the treasure, they're the dungeon masters of the soul—I know that from Richard Wagner, he whispered to me. Dragons breathe fire.

Be careful.

* * *

I fell ill in the new year. Scarlet fever, which I'd had as a child and next to no one ever got twice. I was in an improvised isolation unit at the Hôpital Pasteur, burning up in a glass chamber with bedsheets hung on the walls. There I was, in the heart of Paris, vegetating in Snow White's coffin. My father made the trip because I was hallucinating, and hospital staff feared the end was nigh. He had to stay behind the glass.

Horowitz tried to sneak in a radio, without any luck. My wife threw a fit, he groused. He sent fresh tangerines imported from California, crystal jars of jam, glossy boxes of pralines, pineapples nestled in lined baskets, and letters. Under no circumstances can you let anyone find my letters! he warned constantly. Under no circumstances! His fear was justified in some cases. I want you to get rich again, Horowitz wrote. Make a lot of money and save it up for me. Stuff even a nun would understand. He told me about seeing gay friends. But replacement doesn't come into question, he stressed, otherwise it would be a trade. That's impossible and should stay that way. Every letter closed with instructions to reply immediately and destroy the note. Naturally I did the very opposite. I had time—more time than I knew what to do with—to read each letter thoroughly. Then came the shock: Horowitz saw straight through me. I understand entirely, he wrote, that it's torture for you to be laid up. How horrible, to be alone without anyone there to admire you.

He knew a thing or two about butterflies.

The foundation of our friendship, he repeated time and again, must remain our work at the piano. As a cover, I figured. If you were willing to change your life, you would make tremendous progress. It was obvious what he meant by that. A gigolo like me was incapable of producing stirring music. What I didn't yet understand, because I refused to, was this: a gigolo like me was also preventing Horowitz from producing such music. I didn't buy his vows of fidelity. Milstein had once spilled that Horowitz used to love going to gay bars when traveling abroad. What, just to look? I had a hard time believing that.

When I was finally discharged, the disinfected letters in my bag . . .

He didn't feel well, Donati groaned. It must be the air here in the house.

He drove up the hill in Küsnacht more slowly than necessary, as if trying to delay their arrival.

No, never, Donati finally said. It's a stone's throw from my house, but it never occurred to me to drive up here, despite knowing about it.

It was a house with shutters, built on the hillside in the late twenties or early thirties, where Kaufmann instructed him to stop. 33 Schiedhaldenstrasse. Thick, established ivy created a glossy green barrier against curiosity.

They got out and stood across the street. The Swiss flag had been hoisted in the yard.

The house didn't suit Mr. Nobel Prize winner, Kaufmann said. He called its construction dilettantish and the walls ludicrously thin, although the architect was a star in Switzerland at the time. The draftiness evidently upset Thomas Mann's digestion, and he whined that the layout of the study hindered his creative impulse. Everything was too cramped, too cramped. His wife regularly had to chauffeur him to Röhm Cigars at 46 Bahnhofstrasse in Zurich, where he bought his long Carusos or Khedive 12s. Their fumes helped him endure it all, maybe even himself. His two youngest, who still lived at home—Elisabeth and Michael, or Medi and Bibi—liked the house.

Kaufmann pointed toward the upstairs. I can still see the four of them standing there, behind the white railing. Katia Mann and their daughter wearing shirts and ties, flat, heavy shoes, bulky pleated skirts, and sweater vests, which were called something different back then. As far as I was concerned, Madame Professor—as we were expected to address her—didn't need the sartorial crutch. She already looked like a man, moved like a man, and even sounded like a man.

Donati gazed up at the house as if he expected the couple to appear on the balcony. I've seen photos of her when she was younger, and she was quite stunning.

Yes, a minion with fiery eyes and lots of promise.

He could scarcely imagine such a transformation, Donati commented.

But the wives of gay men nearly always grow more masculine over time. Proust saw it, Kaufmann said. I don't remember which part, but he writes about it somewhere in *In Search of Lost Time*. Women will gradually and unwittingly adopt male traits, even if they didn't have any to begin with, in an attempt to appeal to their husbands by means of mimicry, just as some flowers will take on the appearance of the insects they hope to attract.

From his rigid bearing, it was obvious Donati was not yet convinced. And you say you could already sense that back then? he asked. Thomas Mann's diaries hadn't been released yet, meaning the public didn't know he was gay, or rather, a pederast.

An upstairs window opened and a woman in a house dress began cleaning the glass, all the while peering over her bare arm at the strangers on the street.

Donati turned and climbed into Kaufmann's old Peugeot. Kaufmann told him about Medi as they drove on. In the fall of 1933, she had enrolled at his secondary school, the Freies Gymnasium, which was already co-ed. She was two years younger than the rest of them, clever and quick but awkward, and happy to let people cheat off her in Latin. There was nothing very girly about her. At home she'd told them Nico would marry her on the spot. He was invited over and accompanied Medi's brother in performing a viola sonata he'd composed. Thomas Mann was as unimpressed by the sonata as he was taken with the handsome pianist Nico. Shortly before the Manns moved to Küsnacht, Nico had read *Death in Venice*. The story of Aschenbach's attraction to boys could only be told that way by someone who knew how Aschenbach felt, he told Medi. She was outraged and things got loud. It was the first time he saw her angry. It was utter nonsense, what he was saying. She knew her father very, very well.

They hadn't lingered on the topic of Thomas Mann or returned to the five feet of pink shirts.

Back in Zurich, they ate in Kaufmann's living room, plates of Gruyère with pear and rye bread on their knees, paired with a Ticino Merlot. Kaufmann had selected the wine as a nod to Donati's origins, but he didn't seem to notice. They heard each other bite and chew and swallow. In the background Horowitz played Beethoven—*Appassionata, Moonlight Sonata, Waldstein*—in a recording from the fifties.

So he did play Beethoven, Donati exclaimed out of nowhere, following the final chord.

When it came to music, Kaufmann said, he was willing to acknowledge, admit, and correct a mistake. But only when it came to music.

He approached the bookcase and pulled down one of two identical volumes. *Thomas Mann Diaries 1937–1939* was printed on the spine. Kaufmann had marked a spot with the ribbon. Here it is. On February 19, 1938, he wrote something I'll never forget. The only reason I bought the diaries from his pre-war years in Switzerland was to see if he mentioned me. And then I made this discovery. He faltered, then began to read. *While sitting at the table, we established that we have been married for thirty-three years. The shock, the vertigo it unleashed: this life—I said I shouldn't care to repeat it. The pain had simply been too pronounced.*

He closed the book. I've made up for many of my mistakes, but there's one I saw too late. It might seem secondary, but it wasn't. It concerned Wanda Horowitz.

Donati waited expectantly, his head propped on his fists.

Let's say you were appearing on stage dressed as a woman, like my friend Tiger Lily, for instance. What's the first thing you would grab from the costume designer?

Wig, high heels, red lipstick, and long fingernails, ideally red, Donati replied.

Kaufmann was pleased. Yes, you see, Katia Mann never wore makeup or nail polish and kept her nails trimmed very short. She'd given up. Wanda Horowitz always had red fingernails. It's crazy, if you ever stop to think about it, that we can look at a person, even one we're close to, without really seeing them. We see a red splotch on a painting and wonder what the artist was trying to say. I never wondered what Wanda's red nails were trying to say. *Too late* is tragedy in two words. It was too late by the time I realized what those red nails signified: Look, everyone, I am a woman, and I want to be a woman, and I want everyone to know that.

He swallowed.

I should have been warned.

VIII

❧·❧

It must have been the southerly wind—which had cleared the skies—making people on the street smile for no reason, something you rarely saw in Zurich, much less on an unseasonably cold Wednesday in April. At nine thirty, Kaufmann entered the kitchen with warm *Spanisch Brötli* pastries. He knew from experience that butter, even in puff pastry form, tended to cheer people up. Donati watched him wearily. It looked like he had smeared grayish blue eye shadow around his eyes, and Kaufmann recalled that his father had said this often indicated a deficit in vital substances. It was anyone's guess what *vital substances* were, but in Donati's case, the diagnosis seemed to fit.

Still tired?

I slept poorly and had terrible dreams. You wouldn't believe how terrible. It was too soon, going back to my house.

My mother would often say that when I was young. It's too soon, she'd say when something hadn't yet healed. You need to give your wounds time.

The sunlight flooding the kitchen was fluorescent and revealed that Kaufmann did not monitor his cleaning lady very closely. The men were anxious to get outside. Kaufmann led the way without hesitation.

The lake came into view. Where are we going? Donati asked flatly.

You ask as though anything would be too far, Kaufmann responded, but today's about me, so only I can say when we've reached that point.

A wrought iron gate separated the estate at 17 Seefeld Quai from the street; it was the kind of gate that would have made Donati's mother cross herself and his own knees buckle at age thirteen or fourteen. Beyond the gate, a manicured lawn edged with a ruler, the embankment artificial and sym- metrical, and broad steps placed precisely along the central axis. The steps led to a minor palace for major patricians, with a view of the promenade and Lake Zurich, but more importantly, on view from the same.

Built of Ostermundigen sandstone in 1913, Kaufmann said, for Doctor Fritz Ernst, engineer and politician, a man perfectly content behind closed doors with bread and but- ter, beer, his harmonica, and nary a God, but outwardly as *nouveau riche* as this place. My maternal grandfather. We moved in upstairs the year before I met Horowitz. My grandmother had died in 1936, and the first floor was plenty for Grandfather. It turned Horowitz on to know that I came from such an ideal, polite household, the way other men are turned on by women who went to Catholic girls' school.

A sign by the entrance read *Johann Jacobs Coffee Museum*.

Donati tapped a finger on *Jacobs*. And how did they become involved?

Inheritance dispute. The others wanted to sell, and the coffee people put in the highest bid. Right up there is where it happened, in the summer of 1938. It was like a bomb dropped on a peaceful, sunny day. We were having lunch. The windows were open, because it had gotten hot at the end of the first week of July, and we were grateful for the lake breeze. As always, my father had switched on the radio for the one o'clock newscast.

New laws to eliminate Jews from German cultural and economic life. A conference in Évian to address the refugee problem with thirty-two countries in attendance, including twenty-one from the Americas, nearly all of whom refused to accept any Jewish refugees. My father, mother, sister, and I stopped spooning our bouillon for a moment. Each thinking the same thing, each thinking of him and that Switzerland should be fairly safe territory. It felt as if we were holding hands like we had earlier, after saying grace. The next news item described a recent wave of arrests in Germany targeting homosexuals. German propaganda called them repulsive and subversive boy toys. *Boy toys.* Sounded to me like the propagandists were lechers themselves, they just didn't dare. A few days earlier, in a referendum on July 3, the Swiss had adopted a new penal code that decriminalized homosexuality. I think the Swiss marveled at their own decisions sometimes. I spooned on, staring deep into my soup, whatever it took to hide the fact that in my mind, I'd returned to Horowitz, only alone this time. He had shared his concerns regarding my lifestyle in Paris with my father, but only mentioning the women. It seemed Volodya wanted him to chaperone me, to keep the unwelcome competition at bay. Finally, the weather forecast . . . then came the announcement: And now, a recording in remembrance of the pianist Vladimir Horowitz. In that moment, the news of his untimely death at age thirty-four reached us from Paris.

I ran to my room, tripping on the stairs. In my desk drawer, beneath Brahms waltzes, were his letters, the last one he sent me, from Bagnoles on June 30, lying on top.

Kaufmann reached into his jacket pocket and unfolded a few light-blue sheets of paper. I don't want memory to fail me, so. *My doctors here have the opinion that I am very healthy and even especially robust in my nature. What I lack is discipline in my work. The poor teacher has been influenced by his student.* Kaufmann moved on to the next page. Horowitz announced he was headed for Gstaad, staying at the Palace Hotel, really far too much pomp for him, but the Milsteins owned a chalet nearby, and he'd be alone in his suite.

He was firmly resolved, he wrote, to lead a healthy life that built him up. *No more medicine!* he wrote. I was meant to replace the pills. Kaufmann ran his index finger down the page. Here it is . . . I was the only one who could help him more quickly *really get back into shape*, and that must make me *really proud*. Look, right here: *really proud*. And then— Kaufmann turned to the last page—he declared he would be returning to the stage that very year. *My first concert is officially set for October 1.* His thirty-fifth birthday was slated as a rebirth-day. Fine, it was ultimately a question of belief.

Kaufmann carefully folded the pages and returned them to his pocket. It was time for his resurrection, high time. Horowitz had been buried, buried alive in rumors, and not just about his physical condition, gastric ulcers or some life-threatening illness, presumably cancer. Suicide had also been mentioned more than once. I could suddenly smell his cologne; he must have been standing right beside me, but there was no one there. Perhaps it was wafting up from the letters. I said it out loud, to make it more real: Horowitz is dead. The sentence felt hollow, like a hollow nut. Try it again: Volodya is dead. Hollow, completely hollow, nothing inside. I was trying to give physical form to the horror, in order to believe it. I stripped off my clothes in broad daylight and lay naked in bed, feeling him beside me, that pale, almost hairless, utterly unathletic body with sensitive skin, and said out loud, Now he's nothing but ashes in an urn. Nothing but ashes. I wasn't scared. Any second now, Volodya would step out of the bathroom.

Sudden death, Donati said, drives everyone mad. There's an absurdity to it. Still, it's what most people want for themselves, albeit late in life and ideally in their sleep.

Are you most people? Kaufmann asked.

I thought today wasn't about me, Donati responded.

Kaufmann could not tear his eyes from the upstairs window to the far left. His window. Forty-eight years, yet not a single moment had passed. It wasn't the things he'd said or that may have been better left unsaid that troubled him back then; it was the things he hadn't said and hadn't asked.

Regret.

Did you just say *regret?* Donati asked.

Yes, regret. I had always had a good handle on it. No one could do regret like me. Even as a boy, I'd move churchgoers to tears with my kneeling and prayers, then toss buttons into the collection plate. Now, though, regret had a handle on me. It was whistling and wouldn't stop, like my grandmother's tea kettle. She couldn't hear it in her old age, while the rest of us all screamed, Can't you hear that? Turn it off. It was the other way around now. No one could hear the whistling but me, and I cried, Turn it off.

There were some compromises he would make, Horowitz conceded in his final letter, but only those worthy of him. It hadn't escaped him in Paris that I had my fun in what he considered the demimonde, with third-rate actors, nude models, revue dancers, and *diseuses.* In another letter, he called them streetwalkers, as if they could be bought. I never had to pay, which I'm sure he knew, but maybe that made it worse.

Did Horowitz really write *worthy compromises?* Donati asked.

Yes, he wrote *worthy,* and I'd missed it. After his death was announced, the word jumped off the page; it was a foreign object that couldn't be purged. He had felt debased by my affairs. Was that reason enough to kill himself? If compounded with other reasons . . . he had plenty of reason to be afraid. As a homosexual and a Jew living pretty damn close to our German neighbors. As a pianist who planned to return to the limelight after a lengthy hiatus and began shaking at the very thought of it. As a queer who was afraid of being outed and forfeiting any hope of a professional future to his wife and father-in-law. Fear comes from constriction, my grand-father always said. It constricts your vision and prevents you from finding the way out. It's why he spent his life railing against the church with its talk of sin and threats of hellfire.

Would that he'd been my grandfather, Donati commented.

There was no reply to the telegram I sent to the Palace, so I called. Monsieur Horowitz had booked a room but unfortu-nately not yet arrived. No, no message. I thought I might lose my mind for the whistling. Same thing the next day. Suicide was the worst possible notion, because it made me complicit and filled my head with images. Necktie noose under the Pont Neuf? A puddle of blood and bones at the base of a Gothic church tower? Poisoned in bed? Fully clothed in crimson bathwater? An accidental death would be preferable, but best would be a heart attack or stroke. When it comes to death, most of us are unspeakably selfish. As far as our own demise is concerned: make it snappy. As for other people, though: please be sure to allow plenty of time for us to make amends. We prefer crying with a clear conscience.

There was nothing on the radio or in the papers regard-ing the cause of death. The first obituaries appeared on Saturday, July 9, and wouldn't he have loved to read their praise. On Sunday, July 10, we heard on the radio that Hitler had ordered Munich's synagogue be destroyed. Horowitz had been superstitious, and now I was too. On Monday, the eleventh, I finally fished an express letter out of the mailbox.

From Wanda?

No, from him. He was at the Milsteins' when he learned of his own death on the radio. The canard had evidently traveled from London to the newsroom at *Le Figaro*. Tragicomic, he wrote. Effective advertising, although he'd have preferred something less tacky. Still, he was elated. He had never felt more loved. They'd observed a moment of silence at the Conservatoire de Paris, people were crying in the streets, and since the error was made public, he had been showered with attention. Flowers, telegrams, calls from a thousand and three friends and admirers. People love me, people love me, everyone everywhere loves me, and loves me best. He was swept up in the rush. He was ready now—for me. Gstaad, Palace Hotel, eighth floor. He had booked a room for me down the hall. A piano was being delivered on Tuesday.

They both gazed at the house at 17 Seefeld Quai, which offered no sign of life, let alone an answer. Still, Donati could not take his eyes off the house and off the window, behind which the man beside him had lost his levity after receiving news of an unexpected death. And then returned to concocting lies for his father and titillating lines for the next letter to his lover.

Horowitz had warned me, Kaufmann said. My exciting life in Zurich was probably better for me than sitting around with him in Gstaad, he wrote. But he tacked on a question mark after the exclamation point at the end. The letter was full of warnings that ended in both question marks and exclamation points. It was very quiet there, he wrote, hardly anyone around, but the climate at four thousand feet was so good for you, the air simply marvelous. He always talked about the air, which held less interest for me at the time than a building loan contract.

The off season in Gstaad seemed to stretch out endlessly. The skiers were gone, while summer tourists had yet to arrive.

What made you go, despite his warnings? Yearning? A guilty conscience? Or relief that he was alive?

The feeling that I had almost thrown away a huge chance, the chance of a lifetime.

And what chance was that?

First, to become a fly in his amber. People like us can only dream of posthumous fame. My existence was like the house we're staring at now. For those who see only the out-side, enviable, but meaningless on the inside, bored with itself. Of course it was also the chance to ask what I had failed to before. I didn't understand where his radical self-doubt came from, his insecurity, and then that need of his for fidelity, an alien term to young gays, one they thought only straight people used to describe their dull sex lives. It must have been tied to his family or his past, something he'd never brought up unprompted. I tried to broach the subject once, but Horowitz quickly shut me down. His only brother was fourteen years older, he said, a stranger, while his sister was unimportant, his mother happy, his father successful and content.

So I turned to Milstein. As usual, he had withdrawn with his wife to their chalet in Gstaad.

While Horowitz practiced on Milstein's Steinway, I got to work. Milstein was familiar with the Gorowiz family—only Vladimir went by Horowitz. His mother, a talented but overwrought pianist and spoiled daughter of privilege, grotesquely made up in her later years, and his father, a well-read, well-heeled electrical engineer and businessman with an air of the elite eccentric. Then the revolution came and they lost everything overnight. The business nationalized, home destroyed, furniture smashed, jewelry ransacked, sheet music, books, violins, and piano thrown out the window.

Donati clung to the gate. He could see it play out, the upstairs windows flying open, treasures of bourgeois culture dumped like sewage. It hurt. He groaned.

Yes, Kaufmann said and groaned along with him.

The entire Horowitz family was herded into a two-room apartment in a lousy neighborhood on the outskirts of Kiev. It was around that time Horowitz decided to leave Russia forever. His sister, his closest confidante, was a great pianist as well, whose marriages failed and career foundered. One brother was shot in the revolution, while the other, not much older than Volodya, hanged himself soon after in a psych ward. A year after her dear Volodya left home forever, his mother died miserably. His father withered away to a nobody in Moscow, married a younger woman, and threw his son into a rage during a visit to Paris by showing him a picture of his stepmother. The Soviets, Milstein assumed, had held the young wife hostage.

Milstein knew for a fact that Horowitz was born in Berdychiv, and not in Kiev, like he told everyone. No, no. In Berdychiv. In every interview he said, I was born in Kiev. And why was that fact so embarrassing to him, that he denied it? Wanda said it was because Berdychiv was all Jews, which everyone in Russia knew, and as a self-made Jewish businessman, Volodya's father disdained those *shtetl* Jews.

Did Horowitz inherit that arrogance? Donati asked.

Kaufmann fell silent. Shall we head back?

He needed a good thirty feet, and he took it slowly.

Inheritance. My grandfather always said original sin was the church's attempt at blackmail. The only original sin I know of is the fact that children inherit the very things from their parents that they should cast off. Or want to cast off, because these things cause them suffering too.

It must be some inexplicable feelings of guilt or inferiority that made Volodya lie, Milstein speculated.

Inexplicable? Nonsense! Milstein's wife interjected. If Kaufmann is looking to understand Volodya better, he has to meet Toscanini and Wanda's family. That's all I'll say. No, I withhold from commenting and suggest you do the same.

Guilt.

Kaufmann stopped walking. Maybe it's time to stop using that word.

Those who needn't feel guilty are usually the ones who do, whereas those who should, don't. I didn't. The parents lodging at the hotel had beautiful, bored daughters in tow, and Horowitz did actually like that I could do it the normal way too. I skated down the hallway in sock feet every night, back to my room, the cheapest at the Palace, but still too expensive for my father. It felt fine lying to my father, telling him a lower price, while Horowitz covered the difference. I did him good, you could see it. One morning, he came to breakfast in a pink shirt. By the way, where did you have your pink shirts made?

Custom-tailored in China, Donati replied.

IX

❦

The nude woman lay harshly illuminated on an operating table, her body lifeless, pallid, and vaguely iridescent. Wrists and ankles bound with straps. A thin cloth covered her loins and pubic mound, the dark hair visible underneath.

Kaufmann had pulled the gold-framed, horizontal format painting from a basement shelf, freed it from its carefully taped plastic covering, and laid it on an old ironing contraption.

This hung on the wall above my parents' bed. I never understood why as a child. The picture repulsed me, sparked a physical aversion within me. My father's being a physician did little to explain why he needed something like this in his bedroom.

Donati spoke quietly, as if someone might overhear him down in the basement. It doesn't seem that great a stretch to suggest sadomasochism. This appeared to amuse Kaufmann. It's difficult enough, as you know, to imagine your own parents having sex, even garden-variety, and as for . . . let's call it highly specialized sex, well, that goes beyond the pale. Was it Freud, or someone else, who penned the expression *bodies in the basement*, like skeletons in the closet? Terrific, whoever it was.

An hour later, the Peugeot passed the sign for Tribschen and approached a white house on a green knoll overlooking Lake Lucerne. Three floors of harmony topped with a hipped roof, surrounded by meadowland and flanked by poplars. The April sun broke through two clouds and shone a spotlight on the façade.

Beautiful, said Kaufmann.

Too beautiful, said Donati. The Japanese commit suicide in those places that are too beautiful.

Good thing we're not Japanese. Kaufmann rolled down his window, sniffed the air, and listened. No more chickens. Too bad; they did well here. The roosters were locked up in August of 1938, though, so as not to rend the *Siegfried Idyll* with their crowing. Toscanini would have throttled them with his own two hands. His nerves, oh his nerves, like rubber bands stretched to the breaking point! Horowitz complained. Today's politics make him sick, and he's infected me. It's not good for me, I should be thinking about me, about my health and my comeback this fall, about me and my music and nothing else.

Horowitz left Russia to escape politics, which was easier to do in the West. His father had been swallowed by the gulag shortly after returning from his distinguished son's European tour, reason enough, evidently, for the Soviets to suspect espionage. He deteriorated in the camp like a rotting tree in a swamp, his sister had written. She sent Volodya the same message over and over again. I learned that from Milstein, certainly not Horowitz. He tried to forget, and it worked—almost. It happened in Paris . . .

Donati parked at the edge of the gravel square, beside an eight-cylinder with Zurich plates, which stood out among all the Germans in the lot. Donati carefully cracked his door, and as he did, the car door beside them opened. A deep, willfully soothing *Excusez moi* came from the left, as if someone were artificially lowering his voice. A gray-suited backside was all they could see. Then came that practiced, calming voice again, *Excusez.* Donati froze, shut his door, and turned his head to the right, to face Kaufmann. What about Paris? I'm not leaving the car till you finish.

Horowitz was in his suite, and we had the place to ourselves for half a day. Wanda was being fit for new hats, suits, gloves, and evening dresses, and he received me in the dark, lying half-dead on the sofa with a damp cloth on his forehead. Unbearable headache following lunch with Toscanini.

Too much wine? I asked.

Too much politics! Do you know what he said to me? A politically weak-willed musician is a bad musician.

There was little Horowitz would let stand in the way of his musical prowess, but what Toscanini now demanded of him was the very thing he had avoided in order to be an exceptional musician: to allow political truths into his life. Toscanini had once publicly declared that, should he ever decide to commit murder, Mussolini would be his first choice, followed by all the hangers-on and cowards, one after the other. But as this would make him a mass murderer, he'd have no time left for the baton. He'd been on the blacklist since.

Horowitz was paralyzed that day in Paris and the following day too. He was still dragging his feet, smashing glasses, and refusing to eat or play piano after three days, so I gave him an out. Whereas what Toscanini said might apply to normal musicians, I explained, it scarcely applied to a Horowitz.

Donati checked the rearview mirror before getting out.

The pavement in front of the house was hushed; the poplars rustled and a blackbird sang languidly, but Donati stood at attention, as if expecting an unpleasant encounter. Kaufmann's right arm described a wide arc. They built an elaborate wooden structure right there—Swiss carpentry, that would still be standing today. The concert conducted by Toscanini on August 25 was the crowning moment of the newly founded Lucerne Festival, the moment of its birth, really. It was his festival, his anti-Salzburg, but most importantly, his anti-Bayreuth. I think he'd have devoured Winifred Wagner with a fork and knife, if given half the chance. The first part of the concert closed with the overture to the third act of Wagner's *Meistersinger*, while the highlight of the evening was the *Siegfried Idyll*, performed in the very place Wagner had composed it almost sixty years earlier, upon the birth of his scion, Siegfried. Toscanini knew exactly what he was doing. Tickets were four times the regular price and sold out in a day. Horowitz had invited me as . . . let's call it a family buffer, which to me came as a welcome thrill. I felt like a bridegroom getting a first look at his future relatives. I would naturally work my magic on the women. Kiss the hand you can't bite, my grandmother had taught me. Impeccable manners are a Trojan horse for penetrating any female fortress, particularly when the overlord is a macho.

Three bizarre birds emerged on the red carpet here, to the right of the front steps: Wanda's sister, Countess Wally Castelbarco; Toscanini's wife, Carla; and Wanda herself. Wanda and Wally strutted out in cork buskins and feathered felt caps, while Frau Toscanini was the ornamental duck of the flock, waddling around in low-slung mules. Sonia was a damp little chick glued to her aunt's hand.

The steamboats on the lake are prohibited from sounding their horns this afternoon, per my father's instructions, Wanda told me. No one's ever managed that before, or even dared try. At that very moment, we were interrupted by the sound of a keening horn, probably a car horn, that kept going and going and wouldn't stop. Horowitz burst into laughter, a seven-year-old getting his first dirty joke. Wanda slapped the back of his hand; that woman could switch off his laughter like switching off a lamp. His student, she told her mother and sister by way of introduction. I am under constant surveillance by the family, Horowitz had complained. The two women sized me up like I was a military volunteer. *Bello*, said Frau Toscanini and turned away. *Troppo bello*, said Wally and turned to Sonia. Wanda reached for Horowitz's neck with both hands, expertly undid his bowtie, and retied it. All three Toscanini women turned their backs to me; only Sonia peered through the fence of legs at her *Monsieur blanc*. I was outside, barred from the clan without knowing why. During the concert, Wanda sat between Horowitz and me, keeping their arms linked from the first note to the last.

Kaufmann and Donati rounded the building to the lawn on the other side.

During intermission I strolled about alone, ears pricked up behind the many tuxedoed or silk-dressed backs; the grass smelled of perfume, the summer of cigars.

The Italians had already confiscated his passport, and that summer they were after him again. They had put a bounty on Toscanini's head after a phone call—bugged, of course— in which he described antisemitism as medieval idiocy, thus making Mussolini an idiot. At the prompting of *Il Duce*, a panel of professors released a report that Jews were not of the Italian race, and that Toscanini was an honorary Jew. Mussolini's hounds knew Toscanini's license plate numbers. Were there any here, nosing about?

As though he had a pistol in the other hand . . . The musicians, like soldiers under their commanding officer . . . And to think he stands by the Jews . . . He isn't one himself, is he? . . . They've abandoned all restraint at this point . . . They're even sneaking through dark forests in the middle of the night now, crossing mown hayfields, swimming across the Rhine or Lake

Constance from the Höri peninsula... Toscanini doesn't realize how dangerous... Dangerous for us... Obviously, who else?... It could climb to ten thousand by the end of the year... The Austrians, of course... Did you hear about the resolution passed in parliament last week?... I think the federal police chief is absolutely right, we have as little need for them as the Germans, he said... Artists should keep their politics to themselves... That's right, the Judaization of Switzerland is what the chief said... Close the borders... There are too many here as it is... Besides, an Italian shouldn't get involved in Swiss concerns.

The final chords of the *Siegfried Idyll* wafted into the twilight. While border closers blew their noses, opponents of Judaization clapped their hands raw for the honorary Jew. The same could be said for me: the little man up front climbed and climbed, higher and higher, and stood there before us, a devotional image in resplendent light. The bright white hair framing his chiseled face replaced the nimbus. His black jacket with high-buttoned collar turned him into a priest, and all was well.

A girl in traditional Lucerne garb was ushered on stage, where she curtsied to Toscanini and extended a bouquet of summer flowers with both hands. Toscanini lashed at the bouquet, sending beheaded blossoms to the wooden floor. The girl clutched the bedraggled remains and burst into tears. Toscanini charged up the stairs and into the house, slamming the door behind him. Through the open windows, we could hear him bellowing, I – am – not – a – diva – I – am – not – a – diva – I – am – not – a – diva.

Wanda dropped Horowitz's arm, and the three Toscanini women, a veritable paramedic unit, marched up the emergency lane to the house.

Male divas are effeminate, Volodya whispered to me, and he hates anything effeminate.

The tourists inside on the first floor spoke in hushed tones. No one but Wagner could pull this off, Kaufmann said. Velvet beret, embroidered brocade vest, buckled shoes, silk knee breeches, and a black housecoat with silk lapels. Mere hulls arranged behind glass, but everyone could imagine it was Wagner himself standing there. There was no real need for the framed photo of him clad in these coverings, planted in front of Cosima, who gazed up at him from her seat. Had she been standing, after all, she'd have towered over him— him, the most towering among men.

Too bad they don't show his underwear, Kaufmann commented. Almost all of it pink satin. Hard to come by in stores and impossible to order in men's sizes without a good dose of courage, but his new admirer Nietzsche dutifully scoured Basel's lingerie shops to find nice gifts for his host whenever he visited Tribschen.

Which makes me wonder, for the first time ever, what on earth is meant by *effeminate*.

Donati worried at the back of his neck. He had always slept on his stomach, even back then, at age fifteen. It was summer, and he was hot and the scissors were cold, but their warning came too late. *Effeminato!* he heard his father's voice growl as he awoke, and then he was gone. His long hair fanned out, black against the white sheets.

From the next room, which covered Wagner's revolutionary phase, came that voice again, tuned down to a soothing bass, then that of the attendant, then the voice. Donati stiffened from head to toe and might as well have been next door himself.

Could we step out? he finally said. The air in here is getting to me. Maybe it's their cleaning products.

I interrupted you at *Effeminato*, was the first thing he said outside.

Yes. Kaufmann did not fail to notice Donati grabbing the back of his neck again. Perhaps effeminate simply meant those feminine qualities in a man that his wife forbade him or he forbade himself. Or that he forbade other men from having, because he forbade himself the same.

That evening, I waited with Horowitz in the vestibule of the lakefront Grand Hotel National, on the same street as the Carlton Tivoli, where we had . . . my God, only a year had passed. Anyway. Unlike Horowitz, Toscanini always demanded top-tier hotels with the biggest chandeliers, widest staircases, and most marble surfaces. Frau Toscanini brooded with her embroidery in a solitary armchair. Everyone knew how often her husband had humiliated her with his affairs. Frau Toscanini no longer let it get to her, though. She had clearly made herself at home in her role as the victim and was well aware of the power she wielded over the perpetrator. Toscanini needed his wife in order to maintain his role as a married man, but furthermore, he needed her available to collect payments, smooth out disputes with event organizers, replace destroyed furniture, and pack his bags.

There he was, descending the steps with Wanda.

Horowitz snapped to attention, wiped his mouth, then bowed stiffly, hands clasped behind his back like a butler awaiting instructions. Wanda regarded her husband and her white neck twitched. Was she afraid her husband would betray an effeminate quality in front of her father, and was Horowitz afraid Toscanini would repudiate him? *Effeminato!* You're familiar with the expression. Toscanini was short, didn't even reach my chin, but under his gaze I shrank so thoroughly inside that he loomed over me. He shook my hand, and his was unexpectedly strong and cold, and I felt like Don Giovanni when the Commendatore shakes his hand. *Pentiti!* I heard the Commendatore sing. Repent! *No!* replies Don Giovanni. *Pentiti!* the bass repeats. *No no no!* I heard myself wail. He couldn't hear me, a cowardly Don Giovanni who kept his trap shut. The audience was thus concluded.

I had to catch the train back to Zurich, and Horowitz arranged and accompanied me on my ride to the train station, wheezing beside me in the back seat. The August night was still hot and humid. The station kiosk was closed, the area behind it dark, and there were no travelers waiting on the platforms. Horowitz pulled me into the corner behind the kiosk and asked for a cigarette, then sucked on it hungrily and screamed, as he blew out the smoke, This family is a band of killers. They execute every last person they talk about, including me. It's only in front of strangers that Toscanini shows me off and calls me the next Liszt. I live in constant fear of them. Home is sweet home, is this the expression you use in German? There's nothing sweet about it.

With a squeak, as if his voice were changing, his rage spilled over into sobbing, and he shook so badly, the cigarette fell from his hand. He didn't just put it out, he pulverized it, disgusted, as if it were some sort of ironclad insect.

Then he leaned against the wall, his eyes closed, expectant and thirsty. Your sweet lips, he whispered, your sweet, soft lips.

Do you know the feeling when you get the passenger car all to yourself, when for hours, everything around you has been humming and then just like that—silence? Silence, utter silence, as staggering as death when you stand beside the open grave of a person who didn't even mean that much to you, yet suddenly he's powerful and enormous, both in death and in silence. I opened the window and the curtains flapped in my face, the air smelled of seaweed and August and freedom, and I ran through the day's footage in my mind. The sound was the most important part, it's what everyone had paid for. Mine was a classic silent film, though. The gestures were exaggerated, but it was the actors' looks that said it all, and usually something counter to their movements. I tried to focus the images. Wanda had looked down at her mother from the height of her buskins. Her gaze initially struck me as scornful.

On the surface, Carla Toscanini was the emperor's wife, but everyone was more familiar with his mistresses than with her. Toscanini's wife had lost her honor, and he never returned it to her. But then I thought I detected something akin to jealousy, a painful jealousy, in Wanda's eyes. Carla had held on to her position as Toscanini's only wife; none of his lovers had usurped her, her position was uncontested, and she would die as Signora Toscanini. He would never leave her.

I was certain I'd cracked it. Wanda wanted the same control over her own husband in an effort to preserve her honor as his wife. Then there was the way she looked at Sonia and the way Sonia looked back. The maternal gaze conveyed: What is this girl doing here? She's a distraction and gets in the way. The filial gaze countered: What is this stranger doing here? Wally exuded disdain when she looked at Volodya. Twenty years earlier, she and Count Castelbarco, who was still married at the time, had endured the dispute with her father, who, notorious adulterer that he was, expressed outrage at their adultery. When Wally got divorced and returned to the clan seven years earlier, the gossip columns covered all the family spats. According to Milstein, Wally saw Horowitz as nothing more than a careerist who'd made a calculated choice in marrying Wanda. And then there was the way Horowitz looked at his family, his head lowered. It was the look of a prisoner whose will to escape had been broken. What really killed me was the expression of submission on his face.

Every family that sticks together has a secret: the secret that keeps them stuck. It's rarely love, but more often an eye on inheritance or a rather unpleasant sense of obligation. Most commonly, though, it's dependence, comfort, habit, or fear of loneliness. I was reminded of the picture above my parents' bed. It suddenly suggested itself as the Toscanini family crest. Perhaps they were as defenseless against Arturo as the drugged woman is against the surgeon. Only they climbed on the operating table willingly. They needed the injuries he inflicted. It would certainly explain a few things if it turned out this genius—who was five-three at most, and who suffered the fact that he was five-three at most—had surrounded himself with masochists. Honestly, I couldn't have cared less about the ladies' masochism, but it seemed clear Toscanini had Horowitz under his thumb too.

All alone in the passenger car, I encountered myself as well. It wasn't a terribly impressive encounter. To be adored—that was all I'd ever cared about. Even music was little more than a means to that end. Everything came easily to me and at me, the sympathies, the lovers, both male and female, and enough talent to compose pretty pieces and play nice piano. I had never fought, never fought for anything or anyone, not for the tone of a chord, or the pain in a melody, or a lover. There was nothing great about me. Horowitz had shown me what greatness was, artistic greatness, and to think he would then cower so pathetically before that family? The Milsteins were right: it was the manacles of shame that did it. Volodya felt guilty because he loved men, but had married this woman to further his career. She'll need to have a world-famous name, whoever it is I marry, Volodya had told

Milstein, and hers was the most world-famous. Maybe the marriage was also a ridiculous attempt to heal himself and become normal.

All alone in the passenger car, and silence. I could still taste the last kiss, our longest yet. Volodya had fastened onto me. Was he enlisting me to help him escape with that kiss? He loved me, and he loved Switzerland. Horowitz had to be freed.

Too much sun without a hat, we've seen that before, the conductor commented. It'll peel quick. I had started to glow bright red in the cooling evening.

The lights were still on downstairs when I opened our front gate on Seefeld Quai. It was dark in my parents' room on the second floor, although they could rarely sleep. It was nothing new. My father generally composed his infantry songs in peace and quiet upstairs, while his own father-in-law bellowed pacifist slogans below.

The downstairs windows rattled. *Viva la libertà* from Mozart's *Don Giovanni* was audible from out in the yard. My grandfather was in good spirits, drinking Marzemino.

How many Jews live here? I asked.

Eighteen thousand, he said.

Eighteen thousand, out of a total Swiss population of four million, that's . . . My grandfather's brain was the most reliable calculator in the world.

Zero point four five percent, he said. Why?

I became political that night and . . .

How did it make you feel? Donati asked.

Like a hero, Kaufmann said. I felt kind of amazing, unfortunately. True heroes never feel that way; only the false ones do.

Donati froze with a crunch of gravel as the Peugeot came into view. Too late. The man leaning against the eight-cylinder beside the car had already spotted him. A man in a gray suit and sky-blue tie, whose face seemed made to be forgotten. It was clear, though, that he had not forgotten this particular client.

So it *is* you, he said.

Donati remained silent.

Have you any idea what you've put me through? the soothing voice asked.

Donati remained silent.

The horseman who crossed Lake Constance died of a heart attack upon discovering he had ridden for miles across the ice.

Donati remained silent.

Why did you lie to us? It sounded as if he were asking for directions.

I didn't lie. The truth changed.

Because of him? The man in the sky-blue tie tersely targeted Kaufmann.

No, said Donati. Because of a few minutes of music.

The nondescript man opened his car door, threw himself behind the wheel, and screamed, And the question of guilt?

Can't be solved, Kaufmann responded cheerily. Unlike the problem.

X

⬥⬥⬥

In Kreis 4, no one would shake their head at the sight of a man standing in the middle of the street with his eyes closed in the spring afternoon sunshine, speaking slowly and distinctly, who didn't appear to be a stoner or junkie or drunk, nor someone the men in white coats might soon come for. He didn't even look like your typical soapbox sermonizer, since they rarely wore dark-blue blazers. There must be a reason, passersby shrugged on such occasions in Kreis 4. People there largely agreed that the only scary kind of crazy was never going crazy at all. No one there would ever stop and stare or wonder why this clearly autistic man had a companion. Things were different in Kreis 1, that most sacrosanct of districts. Bystanders maintained a safe distance, far enough to escape unscathed from any potential violent outburst, yet close enough to understand what no one truly could.

I'm going to the loneliest place on earth now. It's awful. No one can help me. It's cold out there, and I've given up hope for closeness or sympathy or touch. Their stench envelops me, takes my breath away as I step into their midst. I have to fight back nausea. The lights blind me, overwhelm me. I stare without seeing at the hundreds lying in wait. I cannot discern a single face. I break into a freezing cold sweat. Behind me, the fear of losing control also lies in wait, an animal ready to pounce. I can already feel its claws, and when it happens, those out there in the dark will show no mercy. It's what they've all been waiting for. The air is charged with their hunger for spectacle. I'm going to the loneliest place on earth now, he said. He was like a robot as he described it, neither raising nor lowering his voice. I stood with him behind the curtain. His arms hung limply at his sides. His hands dangled from his white cuffs like veal cutlets—unthinkable, that they were capable of movement. He had drenched himself in cologne, perhaps in an effort to numb himself or combat the perfumed patrons. Yet he had so looked forward to this day. His public resurrection.

By the time Kaufmann opened his eyes, removed a pair of sunglasses from his breast pocket, and joined Donati in gazing at the portico above the steps, the head-shaking passersby had already moved on. They'd have questioned the soundness of their own judgment to hear the old nutcase now drily explain that, back in 1938, the Zurich Opera House was still known as the Stadttheater. This was not the utterance of a nutcase when made in front of the opera house that had, indeed, once been known as the municipal theater.

Kaufmann turned to Donati. *I am in good spirits again!* Horowitz had written, not two weeks earlier. He downright demanded I come to Bern immediately, take up lessons again, stay with him, at his expense, then return to Zurich together in his car. *With your teacher, with your master,* he wrote. We both knew why he emphasized that. Just as I knew why he needed to tack on a P.S. *I nearly played a Brahms piece last night and remain extremely aroused! Fantastic!* Napoléon supposedly suffered from his infatuation with Joséphine, a woman whose reputation preceded her. Sexual power dynamics are often reversed. The master becomes the slave.

Donati commented that he had recently heard several accounts of top executives frequenting dominatrices in Kreis 4.

That, said Kaufmann, is something altogether different. I call that atonement therapy. Shall we move on? Perhaps toward the Bellevue?

At the very last moment, Donati hesitantly, almost apprehensively, turned around and froze at the sight of a figure like an exotic insect: legs spindly, head encased in a glossy black helmet of hair, neck long and golden, in a voluminous coat like iridescent wings that shifted between bougainvillea and Caribbean blue. This curious creature had presumably emerged from the stage door. Donati called out a name, but too quietly. He called out again, a bit more loudly. The creature paused, appeared to be listening without allowing its gaze to wander, then buzzed away.

Well? Kaufmann asked.

Nothing, said Donati.

His gaze remained fixed on the empty space where the insect had just appeared.

Kaufmann tore Donati away by putting an arm around his shoulders and nudging. They ambled north and Kaufmann resumed his story, almost in time to their steps.

Horowitz felt free in Bern, but above all, invulnerable. Wanda was in preventive detention—he'd sent her to Paris to retrieve his tuxedo, which he hadn't worn in almost three years. I joined him at the Bernerhof, a grand hotel in which time passed as slowly as Bern locals talk. It's no wonder it no longer exists. Do you know anyone with cash—which you really did need to stay there—who embraces such a slow pace these days? The Bernerhof had the discretion of a sanatorium for hysterical or irascible aristocracy. They had white lacquered double doors, the outer door padded on the inside, while the walls between rooms were covered in fabric. He sat at the Steinway in his suite and played what would be the centerpiece of the concert at the Stadttheater on September 26—a scheduling issue had hampered his plan for a symbolic rebirth-day on October 1—Schumann's Fantasie in C. An insane piece, he said. Whether the insanity was in the notes on the page or the mind of the man who dared play it, he didn't say. The first movement opens with a sort of stifled scream. The second movement, in particular the final section, is one of the most feared pieces in the piano repertoire. It wasn't till he reached the final movement, though, *to be played quietly throughout,* that I understood the verse—I think by

Friedrich Schlegel—that Schumann includes as an epigraph. *Resounding in ev'ry sound / in the earth's motley dream / a muted tone there sustained / for him who in secret hears.* Horowitz put everything on the line for that tone. It was a balancing act that made his nostrils flare. I didn't fear for him until he closed the lid of the piano. It wasn't the technical aspect. He said performing this piece was a matter of nerves, and that's exactly what it was. Of all risks for Volodya to take!

Horowitz is returning to the stage.

The announcement had set off fire alarms across the music world. Having arrived in Zurich, Volodya grew more agitated by the day. His tuxedo was only the slightest bit snug around the midsection, he had good color, he was down to just one cigarette a day, and the Fantasie floated gloriously and weightlessly from his fingers, like a vision of a world from yesteryear. Even Wanda said, That's good. I assumed it was a calculated comment. Wanda's That's-Good typically sedated him. Volodya's anxiety was increasing, though, something the event organizer had evidently anticipated. The posters and newspaper inserts read *Benefit Concert for Refugee Children*. It softens the crowd when artists perform for free. The ads deliberately failed to mention that these were all Jewish children. Some were traveling alone, being smuggled overseas with the help of Youth Aliyah to England and the U.S., but in particular to Palestine. Others were the children of refugees, most recently from Austria, whom the immigration police fined for working, thus denying them a means to earn money. Without the border closers and opponents of

Judaization, the concert hall on September 26 would have been half empty. The resurrected pianist was also receiving psychiatric backup: his friend, the violinist Adolf Busch, performed with his quartet in the first half. He had known Volodya for years and arranged his audition with Toscanini in 1933. Horowitz is superb, but he doesn't believe it anymore, Busch argued, which is Toscanini's doing. You're a very good pianist, he told his son-in-law, but nothing beyond. No education, no breeding, no political stance, not even fidelity to the work. And since Toscanini sees Horowitz that way, Wanda does too, and together, they've broken his spine.

Busch thought you could tell by looking at him.

Suddenly the news came: Rachmaninoff would be in attendance. Of all people, the one man as intimately acquainted with the Sickness unto Death as Horowitz, who experienced the same panic when faced with the murderous solitude of the piano. On the eve of the concert, Horowitz decided against the Schumann Fantasie, opting instead for a few pieces by Chopin that did not feature a stifled scream—pieces that were not a matter of nerves.

Even so, the fear paralyzed him as he stood with me behind the curtain, the fear of the loneliest place on earth. I'm sure the stage manager or one of the lighting technicians saw me kiss him. No matter: he marched out on stage.

After opening with the mazurkas, child's play for him, he dried his hands on his big handkerchief, wiping each finger individually. He then placed a fresh handkerchief on the piano within reach and began the *Polonaise-Fantaisie*. A late work. When Chopin composed it, he was frail, mortally ill, yet demanded the utmost of the pianist. It was a dance through the extremes of experience that allowed Horowitz to flaunt everything he had, while revealing nothing of himself. It was a feat that pushed him to the limit, but it wasn't a confessional, not like the Schumann.

As always, his bearing while seated at the piano was distant and calm, but Horowitz played as though his life were at stake. Not until the very end did a little optimism shine through, and Horowitz smiled, as if a miracle had saved him from being executed. I must have appeared drunk as I staggered out of the proscenium box and into the green room after the third encore.

Ten minutes later, Rachmaninoff rumbled in. Pardon has been granted, he said. Horowitz burst into boisterous laughter and galloped around the room. Wanda shot it down with a single remark.

On October 1, Volodya's thirty-fifth birthday, my grandfather was glued to the radio and hoarse with outrage. The Germans had invaded the Sudetenland unimpeded, after Chamberlain, Mussolini, and Daladier had given Hitler permission in the Munich Agreement signed two days earlier, in the name of peace. This means war, my grandfather croaked. This means war, the first step into the abyss. Volodya wasn't interested in all that; he slept till eleven and buried himself in the reviews of his concert. They were like featherbeds.

On October 4, the Federal Council reached an agreement with Germany that stated all German Jews' passports must be stamped with a red *J*. The Swiss government may not have invented this stamp, but they supported it, because they had feared Jews might otherwise sneak in disguised as Christians. Milstein was alarmed. But what was the point in telling Volodya? He would just scream, I'm not a German Jew! And I don't need another Toscanini on my back!

I was glad he was doing as Rachmaninoff said, planning to spend the fall and winter performing in secondary French cities as a stress test for Paris, New York, or London. Rachmaninoff was thinking only of the stage fright he and Volodya shared and couldn't have known he was thus facilitating the very thing he most abhorred—the love between two men. Wanda hated the countryside, so it was ideal for us. Less ideal was that Horowitz had barely any time left to teach, which left us with no pretense for my staying with him for days or weeks on end.

Smiling at Kaufmann and Donati from lampposts, the sides of buildings, and advertising pillars was an upright citizen in a tie and designer eyewear with salt-and-pepper curls. He had been the talk of the town since yesterday, although he was no longer in Zurich. *WANTED* was printed above his portrait, *10,000 FRANC REWARD* below. Shortly after breakfast, this upright citizen—a trained architect and top manager of the local building inspection department—had unhurriedly liquidated four of his employees in their offices with a shot in the head and critically injured another. His ensuing escape was so orderly in its execution that no trace of him could be found.

Kaufmann paused before one of the wanted posters.

There are some perpetrators who avoid capture for years or even decades. Then there are those—often repeat offenders—who seem to be looking to get caught, ideally red-handed. They lack the strength to turn themselves in, but the desire to break the cycle outweighs their fear of punishment. They usually say their conscience got to them, but I think the real driving force is the liberating effect of the truth. Those of us who don't break into houses, rob banks, violate children, or strangle women like to believe these things are alien to us, but just think of Thomas Mann. Maybe that's why he admitted in his diaries everything he concealed and suppressed in real life. Those revelations were meant to be posthumous, he made sure of that. Dropping a bombshell after you die isn't dangerous; it's actually clever, because it reheats tepid interest using voyeurism. You don't need to be Thomas Mann for that, though. Everyone presumably harbors the desire to be recognized. Recognized for who we are or were.

Donati appeared lost in the upright citizen's visage. Interesting thought, he said.

Kaufmann sighed. Unfortunately, one that didn't occur to me until it was too late. Otherwise I'd've been more careful. While I subconsciously yearned for my father to recognize me as Volodya's lover, I made a conscious effort to hide that very fact.

I can still hear my father's voice the time he barged into

my room. It was dangerously soft. So, you think it's fine to lie constantly to your father, is that it? I didn't respond. You think it's fine to spend his savings on your sexual adventures? I still didn't respond. And you think it's fine to rupture the marriage of a great artist and go behind his wife's back, although she considers you a friend?

In his hand was a letter from Volodya, which I had accidentally left lying around.

Kaufmann fell silent. Then he said, It could have been worse. The corpus delicti was fairly innocuous, not one of the letters in which Horowitz went into detail. Worse would have been my father discovering one of my missives, pages upon pages describing my amorous endeavors. Casanova was a slouch by comparison—everyone knows the poor fellow restricted himself to *one* sex. I spared no details. My celebrated appearances at Seebad Enge—my regular swimming spot on Lake Zurich—and intimate encounters in the changing room, the perfect service I provided to both front and back, and the breeding bull qualities of my so-called little animal. Horowitz begged for those reports. He sometimes asked if they were true or invented for his sake, but he didn't ultimately care, either way; it was clear he needed them as badly as the air he breathed. Thank God his references to them always ended in suggestive ellipses.

It could have been a lot worse, but it was bad. That letter forced the virtuous Dr. Kaufmann to look. Look and see what you don't want to see, it said. The artist you revere above all others thirsts for your son.

* * *

Forty-seven and a half years had passed, and now Kaufmann was reliving every last moment.

He couldn't care less how Donati might interpret his silence; presumably he could tell it was that special kind.

Kaufmann's pulse had finally slowed by the time they reached the Café Odeon. It had long since lost its distinctive aroma from the days when he and Volodya, who always kept his back to the room, had sat here smoking and drinking tea. The in-house *konditorei* in the basement, which had thickened the air inside the cafe with butter and vanilla, and the nightclub upstairs, which had sent down a potpourri of eau-de-toilette and cigar smoke, were gone; the gay and the glamorous, the one-of-a-kind characters, bad and beautiful alike, were fewer in number. What remained were little more than generic replacements. None of the staff could even tell you where Mussolini or Einstein had sat, let alone Werfel, Furtwängler, Lasker-Schüler, Toscanini, or Horowitz. As it was, most only knew of Mussolini and Einstein by name. But the marble walls and red leather cushions and crystal chandeliers murmured with the lingering spirit of the past.

What happened then? Donati's baritone jolted Kaufmann from his reverie.

An inquisition was conducted. My father immediately sent an express letter to Wanda, and Wanda immediately called my father. We were given a life sentence, barred indefinitely from seeing one another unless a chaperone was present. They also reached a mutual understanding of culpability: Horowitz was guilty of tempting me, an unscrupulous narcissist, to stray from the right path—the heterosexual one, that is—while I had acted against my natural instincts and become entangled with a man, out of a need to be needed. My father and Wanda seemed to agree that a psychiatrist could shepherd me back to health. Ultimately, my father sensed there was something deeper there and decided psychoanalysis should do the trick, rather than medication or other measures.

The entrance to the cafe was wrenched open, and in flew the exotic insect from the opera. Kaufmann was about to tell Donati to turn around discreetly, but Donati was already staring past him at the wall and groaning. Kaufmann had forgotten there was a mirror behind him. The insect alighted at a corner table, humming a soprano line; it sounded like an aria by Handel or Purcell. Donati groaned again, then stood and walked over to where the pretty insect was humming. They conversed in English, Donati standing, whereas the iridescent creature remained seated. It was brief, then Donati wiped his cheek with the back of his hand, returned to their table, and insisted they leave. Yes, now.

Once outside, he wiped his cheek again with a handkerchief. I was just spit on for the first time in my life, unfortunately with good reason.

And? Kaufmann asked.

Nothing, Donati replied.

They both waited, neither knowing what the other was waiting for.

Kaufmann took the first step toward the Bellevue.

Bill posters had set up their ladders and buckets in front of the Bellevue, by the entrance to the movie theater, and were now stripping off old advertisements and rolling out new. Do you have a sense of what the Grand Hotel Bellevue once was? Kaufmann asked. You're probably too young. Even I'm too young; the hotel was shuttered after the First World War, but my parents still grew misty-eyed when they reminisced about their first rendezvous on the restaurant terrace overlooking the River Limmat. To me, this building was a penal institution. Up there, on the third floor of that tower-like corner, was where my psychiatrist had his office. He perched mutely behind my head and didn't say anything but *interesting* or *I see* or *mhmm*. You wouldn't believe how many variations of *mhmm* he had at the ready, modulating from major to minor, minor to major, in ascending or descending pitch, *con sordino* or *senza*. He asked about my dreams, so I ad-libbed, told him exactly what he wanted to hear. I also brought him my diaries from the time before Volodya, for extra fodder. Still, therapy did have an effect on me. I recorded my dreams on a shorthand machine on my bedside table and attempted to interpret them. It was disgraceful and, at the heart of it, macabre, but now that everything was over, I started to realize who Horowitz really was. I heard loud and clear many things I had basically ignored before. One day we were sitting at that table over there, Toscanini's regular spot, talking about the maestro. A musician who didn't dream would never achieve greatness, Volodya said. Dreams were a musician's reality and people should allow him that, damn it. Toscanini, who pressured him to take a political stance, was one who in Volodya's eyes wrenched the dreamer from his dream, something he considered as dangerous as waking a sleepwalker. The unconscious . . .

May I show you my basement? Donati interrupted him.

The people of Meilen welcomed the diversion. Everyone stared at the Peugeot that pulled up outside Villa Donati, and all were amazed to see the gate open for the dented old vehicle, which looked like a French intellectual down on his luck.

This time the key found the lock immediately. The stairs to the basement were of polished granite. The halogen fixtures illuminated a clinical cleanliness. The door at the far end of the basement was jammed. Donati muscled it open with the weight of his body and revealed a subterranean mountain range.

Nearest them was a hilly region comprised of dusty piles of books. Numerous black covers with gold crosses, bibles or hymnals or prayer books, atop tomes bound in oilcloth, maybe cookbooks, maybe textbooks. Toppled stacks of old magazines spread out below. Vertiginous peaks of pillows, blankets, bedside carpets, store-bought tapestries, and towels embroidered with devout sayings rose in the distance. To the left, foothills of brightly colored olive oil canisters and basket-bellied bottles of Chianti still plugged with nubs of candles. To the right, a ridge of objects wrapped in plastic: Kaufmann could make out devotional statues and collectable teacups, crucifixes, soup tureens, stovetop espresso makers, and casseroles. And at the very back, jagged and steep, glaciers of haphazardly tossed cardboard boxes.

Donati knew these mountains. A chamois couldn't have tread the path through this inhospitable terrain with any greater confidence. He returned from the back with a bundle under his arm and two large albums, which he carried by hooking three fingers under the cords down the spines.

How much time have you got? he asked.

Kaufmann laughed.

XI

❦

SHE DIED with an interminable exhalation. Her swan song poured out evenly. The man who held her heart had left her, forever. *Remember me! But ah! forget my fate!* were her final words after drinking the poison. Queen Dido then doubled over the spot her baroque bodice defined as a waistline. Roses rained down upon the dead figure from the fly loft above the stage, and the audience thundered.

Kaufmann was crying. He wasn't the only one, but wouldn't have cared if he were.

The soloists from Purcell's opera stepped out from behind the red curtain, Dido and Aeneas hand-in-hand. Dido reached into her towering, curly white wig, ripped it off her head, and stood there in a helmet of black hair.

Since last night, Kaufmann had known where it was Donati had first laid eyes on this figure: at the Peking opera in Xiamen. That was more than seven years ago, and at the time she wore the headdress and costume of a Dan Qing Yi, a role described in the program as an *honorable woman who displays grace, even in destitution*. She sang often, though barely opening her rosebud mouth, and moved sparingly in her pomegranate red dress to sounds that left Donati cold: the hollow buzz of a bamboo mouth organ, airy strains of a flute, whimper of a bowed instrument with only two strings, and faltering of muffled drums. As far as he was concerned, it was as far removed from music as sago soup was from soup. He longed for Tina Turner and his mother's minestrone. The Westerners to the right and left of him as well as the rows in front all disappeared after intermission, but what kept him there was Dan Qing Yi, whose voice touched a spot he hadn't realized existed. It seemed to him as though she were seeking protection, his protection, and as though she were directing her gaze, radiant and black, straight at him.

Masticated food debris littered the street outside the stage door. It was dismal and it stank. She accepted his invitation to dinner and agreed to a weekend at the beach on nearby Gulangyu Island. This might be the one woman to convince him of the merits of her sex, Donati thought. She made him feel strong. As she stood at the stove in his bungalow overlooking the ocean, he heard his mother say, Watch a woman from behind while she cooks. If her movements are concentrated and quiet, she'll be fine otherwise, but if she clatters about, spills things, gets distracted, and swears, stay away from her.

Dan Qing Yi was concentrated and quiet.

When she finally stood naked before him, what convinced him was a delicate body, smooth as silk, with supple loins and skin the color of acacia honey.

It was a male body.

Dan Qing Yi smiled at his surprise and explained that Dans were usually played by men.

After a night in which he must have lost two, or even three pounds, Donati learned that Dan Qing Yi loved only men and was thus one of thousands of blossoming flower varieties that had been eradicated in the name of Mao, the most wise. Interrogated, tortured, buried alive in camps and left in shallow unmarked graves, or simply hanged without further ado. A week later, he had twenty-four pink shirts custom tailored by Dan Qing Yi's best friend in Xiamen. Two weeks later, he discovered that Dan Qing Yi was banking on being freed and whisked away to Switzerland. The next morning, Qing Yi woke up alone to an envelope of cash.

By the final bow, Dido appeared without the brocade bodice and skirt, in a close-fitting white batiste slip that hinted at a delicate body beneath, smooth as silk, with supple loins and skin the color of acacia honey. Europe's most beautiful countertenor.

Power and love: two words that ensnared Kaufmann and Donati following the opera, as they sat at the kitchen table in Kreis 4 over chamomile tea. The two should have nothing to do with each other, Donati argued.

Oh, said Kaufmann, really? They always have, though, and tend to find their way back to each other on the stage, in books, films, and in real life. Never ends well. Betrayal, intrigue, separation, war, suicide, sometimes murder.

Or the person in power leaves his dependent hanging, Donati said quietly.

Kaufmann placed his hand on Donati's and thanked him for the catchword. *Dependent* reminds me. It may sound absurd, but Horowitz was dependent on my letters. At the time it seemed that without them, he'd be thrown into some delirium of withdrawal. Write back this instant, make it long, include lots of details, send it express, why haven't you responded? I await your prompt reply with exact descriptions . . .

Kaufmann got up and disappeared into the living room. He returned with a bundle of envelopes. He patiently untied the string and spread out the letters. Nearly all of them bore a glowing red *EXPRESS* sticker.

May I? Donati studied the backs of the envelopes. The sender's name was clearly legible. What about your father? Donati asked.

Volodya had devised a parent-proof strategy. He opened every letter with a page in which he addressed me formally and adopted the tone of a Catholic chaplain. By page two, though, it became obvious that Volodya was jealous and trying to infect me too. Kaufmann picked up a letter, shook his head, looked at another, not that one either, then smoothed out the third. Yes, here's a good example, from October 24, 1938, from the Palace Beau-Site Hotel in Lausanne: . . . *I*

would have loved to perform Brahms for you, for instance, but as
you can see, current circumstances will not allow it. This is why
my first letter was so cutting in tone, because I am now compelled
to study Brahms with others, which is not good for our friend-
ship, as I have repeatedly stressed . . . Write back at once, tell me
how your work is faring, musical, mental, etc. Tell me if you're
playing much Brahms or Chopin and whether it's "mechanical"
or "emotional," and how the little animal is doing. . . . By now
you must realize that your recklessness is to blame for everything
that's happened—I always said you would lose my friendship
the moment our lessons ended. That was why, and I have far too
much decency to be friends in any other context. Things aren't
looking good . . .

It made no difference that Horowitz came to Zurich
and spoke at length to my father and then my psychiatrist.
Recklessness. That wasn't just in reference to the letter I'd mis-
placed. After all, he had given me express orders to destroy
his letters. It also pertained to my, let's say, sexual affairs,
which was all he thought about whenever he wasn't playing
piano. The world was on fire, but it didn't seem to concern
Horowitz. On November 7, we heard on the radio that a
seventeen-year-old Polish Jew named Herschel Grynszpan,
whose parents had been corralled with eighteen thousand
other Polish Jews in Hanover and deported to a refugee camp
in Zbąszyń, had forced his way into the embassy in Paris and
gunned down Legation Secretary Ernst vom Rath. It happened on Rue de Lille, not far from Volodya's favorite hotel.
Not a word about it in his letters. And not a word about

the so-called spontaneous response to Grynszpan's act, after the secretary died. On the night of November 9, SA and SS strike forces torched synagogues, destroyed Jewish homes, ravaged Jewish cemeteries, smashed the windows of Jewish-owned businesses, and arrested around twenty-five hundred Jews. With Horowitz, it was all about his triumphs on tour and hunger for postal diversion. He demanded cheery letters that avoided the tragic at all cost. He was traveling alone and, despite his many successes, his demons posed a threat during those lonely hours.

For those who have never toured as a musician, it's impossible to fathom the loneliness that follows a performance. That of the solo pianist is worst. There are no colleagues, no accompanist. When Horowitz returned to his hotel room, lost, the ovations still ringing in his ears, there was a real danger of his plummeting into depression.

I know, said Donati.

Kaufmann stumbled. Oh God, right. He emptied his glass mug of chamomile in small sips.

Barely twenty-four hours had passed since Donati had told him about the lonely nights he'd spent in hotel rooms while traveling for business, from Budapest to Boston to Beijing. That, unlike others, he'd never been able to pass the time in foreign cities with excursions or benders or watching TV. Culturally things usually hadn't worked out either. Too little he understood, too little he felt, and the moment he stepped outside they tended to descend on him, the—demons, Horowitz had good reason to call them that, he said. They really were demons, volatile spirits. Fuseli's *The Nightmare*, Donati explained, was to his mind the most important painting in Western art. What nonsense to view it as a nightmare. It isn't a dream, he said, the demon truly occupies you—it crouches on you like the monster on the blonde woman's chest in Fuseli's painting and crushes you. The most horrifying part of the picture, he continued, was the horse in the background idly watching the murderous demon with its empty, leering eyes, just like those studying the painting.

The others let it happen, Donati had said. No one comes to your rescue, and eventually you're the only one who can bring about its end. An eternal end.

What about Wanda? Donati asked. Where was she? She could have been useful in filling that void before the demons did.

Kaufmann refilled Donati's tea. She couldn't be bothered to join most of his tours, although she did show sudden interest in the concert in Lucerne, where I might easily have turned up. Because of her, Volodya had to stay in Toscanini's preferred spot, the Grand Hotel National. Then came the call. His voice was hoarse as he summoned me to appear on November 11, the one evening she would be out. I booked my return on the last train of the day, to give us as much time together as possible.

In the marble foyer of the Grand Hotel National, where I had met Toscanini for the first time, Volodya sat slumped in a chair and stubbed his cigarette in the armrest ashtray as

I spilled out the revolving door. Deep lines beside his mouth, dark rings around his eyes, his skin ashen.

He got to his feet with some effort. No, I shouldn't even get settled, he said and fished another cigarette from his case. I lit it for him. He released a cloud in front of his face, and from behind the cloud, he said quietly, but sharply, It's over. We're over.

Over—

Kaufmann fell silent, as though still hearing these words, still stunned by them, almost fifty years later. I once again found myself alone in the passenger car on the way from Lucerne to Zurich. The first time, in August, glowing and certain of success, and now, in November, chilled and coming apart at the seams. I racked my brain for reasons and tried to remember everything Milstein had shared about Volodya. No one loved him as loyally, although no sign of love was returned. No one knew him better. And Milstein had once told me: Volodya might be the last romantic. This coming from a man familiar with Volodya's love of gay clubs, where the action wasn't exactly tame. As far as that was concerned, I didn't take Milstein seriously. The way Horowitz treated property and money, for instance, was far from romantic. When we went out in Paris, he would often loan me one of his precious Fabergé cigarette cases—just for tonight, he would stress. The only gift he'd ever given me was a dark-blue cardigan he no longer wanted. Lanvin, his favorite label. Money was a central topic, now that he'd started touring again. Kaufmann dug through the letters. Here: *I have my rates and will not do charity anymore (I see no reason to).* The Bernoullis had asked him, as a friend, to come down some in price for a recital in Basel. Then here, right below, listen to what he comments: *Out of friendship, they could open their pockets a little if good music is what they want. Otherwise, there are other artists.* He had played for the refugee children for free, but maybe just because he was a kind of refugee himself. It could be he needed the money to ward off existential angst. The collapse of his family, Milstein said, still burned in his mind; moving from the feudal comfort of their patrician domicile to those abject quarters outside of town was a terrible humiliation he'd never forgotten. And then there was his self-doubt. It was possible the money affirmed his own sense of importance and reassured him when he faltered. Whatever the case, it didn't look like romance to me.

The train was already halfway to Zurich, and I still hadn't puzzled out what was so romantic about Volodya. Maybe Milstein meant Volodya's courage in remaining a dreamer, even though society—and not just in Switzerland—condemned such dreamers as saboteurs of reliability and spat them out. Maybe the romance was in his belief that music was something boundless, infinite. Music was his only religion; he didn't need any other. His God lived in music, and when he played well, that was his worship. But none of that had anything to do with me and the fact that he'd ended things.

It wasn't until the train rolled into the city that I stumbled over a contradiction that had long been underfoot. Reading of my exploits stimulated Volodya; he was often aroused to the point where those loaded ellipses were all he could muster. But he'd been hurt by my affairs, and not only when my lovers were those he deemed gutter rats. What seemed to pain him was the suspicion that feelings were involved. And there it was: the romance. Horowitz believed in fidelity, in the bliss of love with your one and only. Bliss wasn't my thing back then; it was too precarious. All I wanted was to get my kicks, and fidelity got in the way of that.

Forget Volodya, think of me as Horowitz, he wrote, and started signing his letters as such. At the same time, he didn't want to be forgotten as Volodya and kept subscribing to chronicles of my sexual escapades for his bedtime stories. He couldn't shake the habit and hungrily demanded new installments. Here, this is a typical example from November 23, sent from the Hotel des Indes in The Hague: *Avoid the tragic*, he insisted yet again. *My little animal is in hibernation, as I am very busy with work. And you? Has your little animal lost its vigor or already found new prey?! No Chopin, no Brahms? And nothing in Jonny's honor?... Respond at length to this question, as light and entertaining letters are all I can take now!*

On December 8, 1938, he wrote from the Hotel Lancaster in Paris and thanked me for my letter. *I enjoyed myself greatly*. France and Germany had signed a non-aggression pact two days earlier, and Volodya thought himself safe in Paris. He had decided to get an apartment in Paris, with Wanda of course, and his enthusiasm at the idea of having his own home was positively childlike. Speaking of children, his own was parked at the aunt's house.

As for being dependent, I was obviously guilty of it too. The scene in Basel no longer did it for me. At age twenty-two, I was back to stretching out my legs under my parents' Biedermeier table. I wanted to become a great pianist, not some small-time music director. I had breakfast with them at seven thirty, lunch at noon, and dinner at seven; someone did my laundry, cleaned my room, and made my bed. My parents covered any shorter trips I had to take, meaning I could only get away with jaunts within Switzerland, where they wouldn't immediately suspect I was headed for Horowitz.

Sneaking around didn't bother me; it seemed the logical response to these disciplinary measures. I had fun slipping my correspondence with Horowitz past my father and sitting down at the table with an innocent smile after one of our phone calls. Horowitz's address changed constantly. As though trying to avoid coming to rest and allowing the thoughts in, he moved from concert to concert, mostly solo recitals, which were the worst for him.

He was booked in Monte Carlo in December, and Wanda insisted they make an appearance at the usual parties and receptions in Paris over Christmas. He had performances in St. Étienne and Lyon in January, in Paris and Brussels in February, then London, plus a few scattered concerts throughout England, and in April came Stockholm and a handful of stops in Scandinavia. He would travel from England by way of Gothenburg, to avoid passing through *the Third*

Gangster Reich, as he called it. Recording with Toscanini—but without Wanda—in London in May, followed by recitals in the Netherlands. He had at least allowed himself a summer hiatus, but he would be back in England in November and December of 1939 and touring North America from February or March until May of 1940.

He never tired of berating me. I should face the fact that the breakup was all my fault, he would say. Just a second . . . Kaufmann found what he was looking for.

Here . . . *Over the 1½ years I was your teacher and friend, I had to be very patient. Your way of living and thinking was often unattractive and alien to me! I told you that many times . . . You'll get older and come to realize what you had with me as a person.* Now look, Donati. He slid the page toward him and pointed at the word *person*. It was underlined three times.

Suddenly Horowitz was taking a moral tack. I didn't understand what was going on. I was, however, relieved to see that he desired me as much as ever and had no compunction about betraying Wanda.

Should we somehow find a way to meet this winter, we'll need to keep it from my wife . . . Have you gotten fatter or thinner? I see you've found a replacement and now play Brahms à la Chopin. Send me details about everything you're playing and in what style . . . It's good for me, because it curbs my need to find someone to play with . . . I'm so tired . . .

His fatigue wasn't just because of touring. Since returning to the stage, he was recognized everywhere he went. Our game of hide-and-seek was now extremely risky and therefore stressful. I couldn't just up and move to Paris to be at his disposal; not only did my father forbid it, my psychiatrist was as fervently opposed as Wanda. I was supposed to—Kaufmann snickered—become normal. Regardless, Horowitz hoped to win over my father. Volodya was planning a two- or three-week vacation in the Swiss mountains in early '39—nothing below three thousand feet, his doctor in Paris had recommended—and Wanda declined to come, because she was busy planning his big tour in the U.S. We could see each other then, Volodya wrote. I was to explain to my father that I was in desperate need of a review, and that this presented an exceptional opportunity. The exceptional opportunity was heavily underlined. On December 27, 1938, he stressed that I was *extremely lucky* to receive his offer, because he was then booked for months. My father didn't see it that way.

In the early hours of January 1, 1939, I dreamed of war. For once, I described it truthfully to my psychiatrist and analyst. This has nothing to do with world war, he said. It's about your own inner conflicts. I scarcely need explain that weapons are phallic symbols.

But my main adversary, the one with the largest weapon and fantastical black armor, opened her visor at the end—it was a woman, not a man.

Mmm, my analyst said.

It was Frau Horowitz.

Mmhmm, he said.

What you said about the phallus can't be true, then, I protested.

Is that so? he asked brightly.

I was furious. The other enemies revealed themselves to be women too, I bristled. All women, and Frau Horowitz kissed them fervidly.

Sometimes, he said, dear old Freud was right when he said our wishes are fulfilled in dreams.

And with that, he concluded our session.

On January 15, 1939, Volodya got his revenge for the fact that my father had declined his offer and I was too cowardly to oppose him. I was, he wrote, clearly in urgent need of psychological care, a process I should undergo without disturbance.

Kaufmann located the letter immediately. *As the only possible source of such "disturbance," I should probably stop writing, as I'm sure it's preventing your psychiatrist from freeing you of me! . . . I agree completely with your father that you should remain at home for the time being, considering that a nearly 23-year-old person or man . . .* Kaufmann looked up and pursed his lips. After the word *man,* he put a question mark in parentheses . . . *who doesn't know where he's going or what he should do, what he loves or doesn't love . . . a "phenomenon" like that demands treatment . . . Please do not defend me anymore, as I do not require it. I know what I gave you, and I will always look back on it with pride.*

Horowitz left no doubt about his thoughts on homosexuality and me. When he first met me in Basel, obviously I'd had plenty of experiences with men already. Besides, he was convinced homosexuality was congenital and not the result of outside influence, but even if the latter were the case, it certainly wasn't he who corrupted me.

I had written him about something my father said, namely that another reason he didn't want me seen with Horowitz in hotels or elsewhere in public was because his past was common knowledge. No idea where he'd heard that, maybe from Wanda or my psychiatrist, who spoke Russian and may have teased something more candid out of Horowitz in conversation. This comment about his past seemed to shake Horowitz deeply. *I don't believe a person of culture can or should be allowed to say such things!*

The story of Vladimir Horowitz, the great concert pianist, and Nico Kaufmann, his first student, was over. That much was clear. It wasn't something a few letters or another clandestine tryst in some hotel room would change either. Volodya said that although I was the melody, the time had come for variations, and they would present themselves in good time. After all, he needed a secretary for the U.S. tour.

I was on my own again, without many laurels to speak of. Abandoned jobs, no personal income, a failed attempt to use Horowitz's help to relaunch my career as a pianist. By that point I was taking lessons here with one of the Frey brothers, both well-regarded professors, but who cared about someone's reputation in Switzerland compared to world fame? How could a halfway decent pianist possibly compare to one who sent audiences into a frenzy? They knew nothing of the miracle of tone, for which Volodya lived and would die.

With all my free time, I wandered around the city and Tonhallen Platz—today's Sechseläuten Platz—where political refugees from Germany and Austria met in hotel foyers, cafes, and bookshops, while just outside on the square, the Frontists, members of the pro-Nazi National Front, held their rallies. Some refugees sought shelter or patronage at Café Odeon or Select, while others begged for a cup of coffee at the Dr. Oprecht Bookshop or the Librairie Française. When I eavesdropped on their conversations, it felt like I was doing it for Volodya. He was gay, and he was a Jew—he would have been among them, had he pursued his career from Berlin or Hamburg, where it all began.

Do you know what today is? my grandfather cried on January 30, 1939, as I was leaving the house. You must. He shook me by the jacket. I remained silent.

Six years ago today was the beginning of the end, he roared. The day he became Reich Chancellor.

When I returned home later, my grandfather intercepted me before I could dash upstairs. His son-in-law didn't give two shits about politics, he growled as he herded me into his living room and sat me down beside him by the radio. Soon, soon. Live broadcast from the Reichstag.

There's one line I still know by heart.

Today, I want to be a prophet again—if the international Jewish financiers inside and outside Europe should succeed in plunging the nations once more into a world war, then the result will not be the Bolshevization of the earth, and thus the victory of Jewry, but the annihilation of the Jewish race in Europe.

Two days later, a letter arrived on Seefeld Quai from Lyon that Horowitz had written that same January 30, 1939. I had to reread it three times, and even then, I couldn't believe my eyes. As usual, not a word about the political situation, but suddenly it was Wanda he wanted to talk about, and only Wanda.

My wife knows everything about me. My wife grants me total freedom, but under no circumstances will she allow a relationship. My wife has known about us for a year, but didn't want to say. My wife has suffered as a result. I love my wife deeply and truly, and I do not want my wife to suffer. My wife does not wish to see you again, even together with your family. I can understand my wife; your father has been unpleasant and arrogant. You are standing between my wife and me.

Then came the real slap in the face: You're calculating, and I want nothing more to do with you.

It was his handwriting, but it wasn't him.

Something wasn't right. The letter ended with a confession. *I need to see you, but can't. I feel for you what I always have. I am brokenhearted.*

I felt nauseous, probably a stomach bug, I lied that evening, then escaped to my room. I locked the door and lay down in bed, naked but for his blue Lanvin sweater, smoked his brand of cigarettes, and drank the vodka he drank with Rachmaninoff.

It wasn't until fatigue set in that the magic word appeared: America.

We're all becoming Americans, Horowitz had reported. The Maestro, his wife, my wife, my daughter, and I. We leave for America in three months and will immediately be under American protectorate, and in three years we'll receive American passports. As far as classical music was concerned, if there was one man that continent belonged to, it was Arturo Toscanini. No one could hold a candle to him, in terms of fame and power and celebrity.

Without Toscanini, things would be hard; with Toscanini as an enemy, they'd be catastrophic. Volodya's wife used the names Toscanini-Horowitz. She wanted both and needed both; the first stood for her inheritance, the second for her current possession, because otherwise she had nothing. Her father had robbed her of music, although Wally claimed that, of the three children, Wanda was the only one with any talent. Toscanini had called her piano playing a disgrace and forbidden her from singing in public.

But how had she won over her husband? I have never loved her, he told all his friends.

The explanation arrived in the mail four days later, composed in Paris on February 5, 1939. Again it was all about Wanda. My wife thinks that, despite your talent, it isn't a Horowitz you need—X or Y in Zurich should be plenty. My wife is a very decent person with high morals. My wife is the leader of my life! My wife understands the occasional affair, but like any woman, she doesn't understand how one can have feelings for another man, or if it should be allowed. My wife sees it as an illness to be healed. My wife will leave if I associate with you. My wife has suffered terribly and almost experienced a nervous breakdown.

Then came the clincher: *My wife no longer wanted to live without me.*

Wanda had threatened suicide.

Warriors know no scruples, my grandfather always said.

Wanda won because she fought with whatever means necessary.

I was a coward. I deserved to lose.

Kaufmann slumped, exhausted, on the kitchen chair.

Donati stood up and kissed him.

XII

❧

THE MEN'S public toilet on Zweierstrasse in the heart of Kreis 4 had been known to them both since childhood. The free-standing art nouveau pavilion looked like the gatehouse to a grand estate, but was originally constructed as a urinal and served as an emblem of the fourth district without anyone pausing to wonder why.

Early that morning, Donati had suggested they walk there from Kaufmann's apartment. His story would flow more easily that way.

God keeps watch over you, my mother said whenever things went well for me, yet again. Top of my class in secondary school. Awarded scholarships. Aced my law exams with distinctions. Full ride for study abroad. I looked neither right nor left. I led an exemplary life, but I wasn't living, at least not like a man of twenty-three. Among my fellow students, I was the only one still living at home, sleeping in the same bed as when he was twelve. My parents were proud, and they were worried. Other people's sons—who came home to Kreis 4 on Sundays for coffee, cake, and old films at the Missione

Cattolica next door to the Church of Don Bosco—were engaged, some already married. I hadn't even brought a girlfriend home.

Right there's where it happened, to the right of the urinal, late one evening. It was someone from the Fourth. I knew him from the past, from our playground days, and it seemed he had exited the toilet right behind me. He punched me in the chest. What's the point of having a dick if you can't even look at it when you're taking a leak? You just stared at the wall. You scared of it, or what?

I was woken the next morning by the sound of my mother sobbing loudly. It came from the stairwell. She stood outside our door, scrubbing, her face bright red and soaked in tears.

Someone had glued pages from a porno magazine to our door. It was gay porn, and it was really stuck on there. She scrubbed for a long time. Once the door—it was a new door, too, early Formica—was white as a Communion dress again, she put on her coat and went to church to get holy water. From that day forward, my mother never looked me in the eye again, even when talking. I often sensed her watching me from the side, but no matter how quickly I turned to face her, she had averted her gaze again.

She loved me more than her own existence, and presumably more than she loved my father. She never let him in on her suspicions. I don't know if he was more likely to thrash me or inflict harm on himself. A myoma developed in my mother's stomach, an enormous tumor that made her look pregnant, at age fifty-two, and she would come home from confession with puffy, tear-stained eyes. I felt guilty. You understand?

Kaufmann quietly started walking and talking, as though he hadn't heard the question.

From the time I started seeing the psychiatrist, the word *normal* appeared at least once in almost every letter from Volodya. If you become normal, in case you are normal, since your father says you're actually normal, you can lead a perfectly normal life under medical supervision, perhaps you'll find balance and the way you think will become perfectly normal. He thought I needed a psychiatrist, whereas he did not. Thank God, he declared, I'm perfectly normal in every regard. Totally normal. Besides, he reasoned, there was nothing he could change, because he was too old.

If there's one thing Horowitz definitely wasn't, it was normal. Milstein had a clear memory of Volodya from before he was even twenty: he would dress up in this monstrous fur coat and long curls, fully made up with lipstick and black drawn-on eyebrows, and strut around Moscow and Leningrad in full daylight. Or he'd wear a monocle and far too many rings, tuck the piano excerpts from Wagner's Ring Cycle under his pillow at night, then have to be dragged from the sailor bars of Odessa at dawn. Eccentric was a label he was used to. In fact, he liked it. To declare himself normal all of a sudden struck me as absurd, both on the personal level, obviously, but also musically. In everything he played, Horowitz summoned the singular beauty that resided in deviation from the norm. Then something inside me started ticking, and the ticking grew louder and more menacing: it was the question of what had led him to this bizarre self-diagnosis. It smelled of fear. Was it the fear of his wife? Wanda censured him for making faces or clowning around. Was it the fear of Toscanini? His father-in-law had scuttled his habit of playing things that weren't in the notes on the page; he hated the effeminate and the look of Volodya's wild tuxedos. There's something feminine to every last one of us, Horowitz now wrote. Every last one of us, even you! He was defending himself furiously against a suspicion I had never voiced, namely that, given the roles we assumed when playing Brahms, his was the feminine character, mine the masculine. Or was he afraid of striking people as not-normal, there in his new home in New York? Society gays were tolerated in clubs and on the scene, or in the audience at the theater or opera, but they were ousted from prominent positions, particularly in the arts world, news that even reached us in Switzerland. Or was Horowitz afraid of a public outing? Switzerland had its fair share of well-situated homophobes—doctors, politicians, publicists, not to mention the Frontists. My psychiatrist and father were bound by medical confidentiality, but the same could not be said for some room service waiter, chambermaid, or hotelier.

As though they'd planned it, Kaufmann and Donati turned onto Bäckerstrasse in lockstep, both lost in thought. Normal. Its substance was depleted, Kaufmann had said it so many times back then. A disposable word. He stopped abruptly in front of a building on the corner, the outer walls tiled at the bottom with two iron rings for dogs by the door, as if it had once been a butcher shop. He leaned his head back. Third floor, on the right, three rooms, antique furniture, good paintings. A friend of mine lived there, lesbian and Communist. She had let Volodya and me use the place during the day a couple of times, but those two visits were more than enough for him; he thought it sordid, even the area. He suspected it was a flophouse for paying guests. Everything's sticky, he said. No matter what you touch, it sticks.

Kaufmann's gaze dropped to the ground floor. Displayed on hunter-green velveteen beneath the skull of a royal stag were firearms of every caliber, interspersed with burnished brass projectiles, vials of gun oil, and tin canisters of gunpowder, which bore a large, easily legible inscription identical to the smaller lettering on the weapons: *NORMA*. Kaufmann snorted. Norma, of all things. Swedish manufacturer they were already selling here back then. Killing is just the norm.

Could I show you what I considered the norm? Donati asked.

Kaufmann had never entered the Church of Don Bosco on Feldstrasse, despite always having lived nearby, save those years on Seefeld Quai. He thought it looked like a train station from the outside; there was nothing remotely churchlike about churches built after the fifties. The door wasn't locked. The chapel was a bit like a train station on the inside too. The walls were hung with murals glorifying the life of the saint. Donati pointed out a boy of about eight in a perfectly ironed shirt and coat, who looked straight out of a

Wirtschaftswunder-era advertisement for zwieback. The lad was sitting on a hamper, an open book in his hands, while his peers, similarly clad in pressed shirts and coats, crouched and kneeled in reverence before him; a haystack towered at his back and a halo gleamed about his head.

That was how my mother saw me, he said.

That makes three of us, Kaufmann whispered.

. . . until the incident with the porno.

Back outside, Kaufmann paused and frowned warily at the dark rainclouds. Speaking of normal: Uncle Hans, the gay uncle, was my mother's brother. Both her father and mine had ostracized him, whereas she never said a word on the matter. I ambushed her one day as she sat at her vanity; we addressed each other in the mirror. Are you disgusted by the thought of Horowitz and me as lovers? I asked her. She slid a hairpin into place, then another and another. Only when I picture you kissing and writing love letters like a man and woman. Only then. As for the feelings, well, I mean, you couldn't possibly . . .

Donati sighed. So you'd lost your halo too?

Absolutely, and you know, Kaufmann said, that's how you can tell we both had Catholic mothers. I once asked Milstein why Volodya's mother never stopped her son from smashing the family porcelain and smearing makeup on his face. She was a Yiddishe mama, he said, and like all of her kind, she felt the only reasonable part of the Jesus story was that Mary, herself a Yiddishe mama, would think her son was God.

What about his sense of guilt? Donati asked. I'm talking about Horowitz. As a law student, I once scoured the Torah for its penal aspects. It states that any man who beds another man shall be stoned.

Horowitz hadn't seen the inside of a synagogue since childhood. He didn't feel like a Jew until he learned of the Holocaust, as was the case for many.

Continue, said Donati.

What do you mean, continue?

With the letters.

That gray morning was just like their first evening. Donati had taken a seat that provided a view of the Steinway and the silver-framed photo of Horowitz. Kaufmann was hunkered over the coffee table, where he had arranged several stacks of letters.

No more thrill, no more pitter-patter of my heart. It used to be I had to retreat to my room at the sight of his hand-writing on the envelope, to be alone with my fantasies and their effects. Now I seized up before sliding the letter opener under the flap. He submitted me to an extreme, almost intol-erable emotional rollercoaster. His tone would swing sharply from torrid and aroused to frigid and aggressive. Here, if you please, words written by the man who supposedly loved me: *You're too intelligent and talented to lead a stupid life, and too stupid to lead an intelligent one.*

It seemed he was alone a lot and, in his loneliness, fix-ated on this ominous notion of being normal. He had even discussed with my psychiatrist and father the possibility of our having a relationship, minus the sex. Unthinkable for Horowitz, but he naturally kept that to himself. Playing Brahms was more than just a code for him. I consider it part of the whole piece, he wrote, and without that part, the piece as a whole has no meaning. In a sonata you have to play every movement; it's all or nothing.

He accused me of playing a single movement from three entirely different sonatas. It was an offense, he said. A betrayal of love.

Love is the mightiest force, I had written him. It knows no bounds. A fat lot I had done to prove it, he bitterly responded. If my love truly knew no bounds, then instead of churning out long letters, I would have come see him in Paris, if only for a few hours. Money wasn't a constraint; it was a cop-out. He would give me whatever I needed. Not for a cocotte, though, meaning whores. For a second time, he aimed the worst possible accusation at me: Every move you make is calculated.

I couldn't stop wondering what or who had convinced him of that. Was it the excessive fawning and success? The ultra-wealthy have a hard time believing anyone could ever love them simply for who they are.

Soon he was begging for mail again; it was urgent, very urgent. How effortlessly I had always served him what he ordered, be it spicy, coarse, or smooth. But I couldn't do it anymore. Dearest Volodya, yesterday I was . . . Dear Volodya, yesterday I had . . . That was as far as I got. Volodya tightened the thumbscrews. In a letter from London in early March of 1939, he threatened—with a veritable firing squad of exclamation points—that if I didn't respond by whatever day in March, I wouldn't hear another peep from him for the rest of my life! Guaranteed! He then provided detailed information about when, how, and where he'd be awaiting me, Wanda-free.

A few days after I received this threatening letter, a true threat emerged. On March 15, 1939, German troops invaded Czechoslovakia and occupied Prague. My grandfather cried and crashed about, while my father shook his head and penned a new infantry song. Blue emergency lights for bathrooms, stairwells, and corridors filled the display windows in appliance shops. Our government had already held a blackout drill, back in June of 1937. They were now starting to consider mobilizing the forces.

Horowitz reported exclusively on his many coups, as well as his plan to retreat to Cannes after his final concert on April 1; he expected me to join. Had he no idea how deeply he'd hurt me? If my father and psychiatrist stood in the way, because they anticipated my recovery—he put recovery in quotation marks—he could easily travel to Zurich later, by way of Lucerne, though sadly only for two days. He had rented a house in Gstaad for the summer. As always, he demanded I send my reply express.

On March 31, 1939, British Prime Minister Chamberlain pledged the support of the United Kingdom and France for the safeguarding of Polish sovereignty. French newspapers described an atmosphere of panic in Paris. The country was ready for war, the papers read, and everyone knew what that meant.

Three days later, Horowitz—evidently unfazed—detailed his sensational performance in Paris and introduced a brand-new theory. He explained that I was obsessed with the idea that he, Horowitz, played the leading role in my life, reasons for this being my immeasurable admiration of him coupled with pronounced homosexual proclivities. I mistook this idée fixe for love, he continued, but in reality, it was a psychologically anomalous attachment—he actually wrote *anomalous*—and I was therefore in need of treatment. His conclusion: *You must do whatever your psychiatrist says*. His rationale: *Your doctor is your Führer!* It sounded macabre, not least because the whole world was reporting on the megalomaniacal celebrations being planned for the actual Führer's fiftieth birthday on April 20. Swiss sympathizers, whether Frontists or Nazis in uniform, were on the street selling pre-addressed greeting cards to Hitler.

On April 6, Horowitz called our house. He sounded nervous, covetous, struggling to keep his composure. He wanted to come to Zurich now, right now in early April.

We were on the phone for half an hour.

Donati spoke toward the piano, as if he feared eye contact might compromise the storyteller's incorruptibility. And that didn't upset your father?

Kaufmann restacked the letters, tied some back into bundles, and rummaged. The onionskin rustled.

You spoke earlier about feeling guilty. My father was seriously ill at the time, had been for two months. Kidney disease. When colic struck, he would just whimper quietly. I had never seen him hurting and weak. I had never felt so close to him. At the same time, they were back, and after I thought I'd shaken them: Hell's torture staff joined ranks with the priests and took up residence in my dreams, armed with their *If you, then*s. If you go to Paris to see Volodya, then your father will die and you'll be condemned for all eternity, they moaned.

I opened the next letter from Paris on April 8. Here it is.

Unfortunately, given the terrible state of affairs in Europe, I must delay my travel to Zurich, because I can't be in Switzerland if war breaks out, but instead must remain here, as my initial paperwork for America is in place, and I would then leave for America straightaway. Secondly, if war breaks out, the people in NY can't know I was ever in Zurich.

Horowitz had informed my father of his planned trip to Zurich, under the pretext of meeting with my psychiatrist. This, he informed me, was the last thing on earth he wanted to do.

The messenger delivered the telegram on April 10: *regret must stay in paris.*

On April 11, the messenger winked as he handed over the next telegram. Those Parisiennes are something else, aren't they?

But I was already reading: *will arrive midnight schweizer-hof basel tomorrow afternoon Zurich.*

I knew my instructions. I was to book a room at the Baur au Lac for four days and inform the hotel manager personally that Horowitz wished to be left alone and expressly forbade his visit being used for publicity.

April 12, 1939 was a Wednesday, that midweek no-man's-land. I always felt lost on Wednesdays. I started waiting for Volodya far too early, concealed behind a Parisian newspaper in the hotel bar. I can't tell you how many times I wiped my palms and the bridge of my nose with one of those little cloth napkins they used to pass out with snacks and drinks. The napkin was damp, but he still wasn't there. Half a year had passed since our last encounter in Lucerne. I stared at the newspaper, but all I could see was the king-size bed standard to luxury hotels, and in it our two naked bodies, which fit together so well, as he always said. Our bodies resembled our hands, his pale, spindly, and thin-skinned, mine muscular, usually tanned, and sturdy. Under the bed, though, the shards of glass he'd strewn carpeted the floor: I was calculating, cold, lusting after celebrity, fake. His accusations were cutting, and my wounds were far from healed. Volodya had stressed the point repeatedly: I'm traveling more than nine hundred miles from Paris to Zurich just for you. My time, money, effort, risk—it's all for you. The least you could do is be in a good mood.

I had talked big about a love that knew no bounds. Now there I sat, waiting, examining my emotions. I discovered I was afraid. Not of him, but of what would happen inside me when we first touched—or rather, that nothing would. What if love had slipped away and I had to pretend otherwise when embracing him? I could do it, I could easily feign affection when it was the price to pay for my own gratification. But what if it made everything worse? Or if I could only pull it off with others?

The hotel manager pretended not to see me and busied himself behind the bar. At this hour there were only a handful of guests seated at the little tables, most reading, scarcely any conversing. You could hear the manager flip something open, followed by a momentary hiss and crackle.

If you've ever practiced a piece exhaustively, tortured yourself with it or been tortured by it, you will recognize it for the rest of your life. Chopin's Étude in C-sharp Minor, Opus 10, No. 4 sparkled in the low light of the bar. My newspaper dropped into my lap and slid to the floor. It wasn't the piece that hit me, it was Horowitz himself. I moved seats to be closer to the record player.

London, March of '36, the manager whispered to me.

Other études followed, then an impromptu. The crackling briefly roared like an open fire. Then came the sound of a single hand playing. It was the first measure of the Nocturne in E Minor. The left hand played solo. I knew every note, but that measure now hung in the room like an imperious, alien question. A fundamental question. And then, like a painful accusation . . .

Kaufmann fell silent.

What happened? Donati asked without turning.

Forget it. Describing music is a fool's errand. Music begins where language fails. How can one expect to transform it into words after the fact? It's better to hear it in your head.

I'm sorry. Donati's voice was husky. Like most classical music, I don't know this piece offhand.

Kaufmann got to his feet with effort and shuffled to the sideboard. There was a click, and a single hand began to play the melody.

They held their breath as the final pianissimo evaporated. Then came another click, the tonearm glided back to its rest with a tap, and both men inhaled audibly.

At that moment, Kaufmann said, Horowitz entered the bar.

From then until that Friday, Volodya and I were in a state— he rustled, stuffed letters back into envelopes, pulled others out, sighed quietly.

In a state, he finally continued, that could explain why, according to apocryphal myth, Jupiter ordered Cupid be killed, after Cupid's arrow blinded two humans to everything in the world but each other. Those shot by Cupid's arrow became indifferent to the suffering, need, and well-being of others, even those nearest them. A danger to social coexistence that Jupiter, as the one in charge, decided to eliminate.

Okay, Donati said, okay, as though satisfied with the comparison, but a grumble of hunger escaped his insides.

Kaufmann went to the kitchen and returned with chocolates.

Fortifying stuff, he said, as Donati pried a white truffle from the box and he selected a dark-chocolate praline. Have you read the *Decameron* by Boccaccio?

All I know is that it was written in the fourteenth century and is considered anticlerical, erotic, and at times pornographic.

The *Decameron* is a collection of novellas that marks the advent of modern Italian prose. The frame narrative depicts ten people gathering at a country estate in Tuscany and sharing these stories over the course of ten days. They had all fled the Black Death in Florence, the Plague. I can't see your face, but I imagine you're yawning right about now. If you read it, you wouldn't be. What impresses me most is Boccaccio's insight that love and lust—even if only elements of a story we're engrossed in for half an hour—can put the fear of death in us. Since Boccaccio, far too little has been written about love in times of danger, epidemics, and war, or when faced with our own mortality. By now, even Horowitz acknowledged that war was imminent. We made love as though for the very last time. Maybe that's why we spent those days so . . .

Kaufmann cleared his throat and ate another truffle. . . . so entranced.

But it was fleeting, Donati said. I mean, love doesn't help long-term against the weight of misfortune.

Nothing does. Kaufmann sounded buoyant. Happiness doesn't last, and the weight of misfortune is something invented by humans who fear death.

That's where you're wrong, Donati said. It's something

discovered by humans who go looking for death, hoping to escape life sooner than nature allows.

Kaufmann was silent. Pity, he whispered. I thought I had . . .

The silence grew, neither man filling it.

This emptiness doesn't frighten you? Donati finally broke the silence.

Silence isn't empty. In music, the rests are as important as the notes. Horowitz loved rests. That's where things really resonate, in the music and with the crowd. Anyone can earn applause, he explained. But the silence before and during a piece, that's the ultimate.

Kaufmann paused again.

Still, let's continue.

On Friday, our second-to-last day, Volodya asked if I would ever leave Switzerland.

Forever?

For a long time.

I stuttered, But it's . . . it's my home.

Home?

He laughed. I haven't had a place of my own since leaving the Soviet Union, and as far as Europe is concerned, it seems it will stay that way. I have spent nearly a third of my life in hotel rooms.

But home is also . . . it's also people, family and friends, I said.

I thought you met my new family in Tribschen, he said flatly.

On Friday afternoon, after Horowitz emerged from the bathroom and, for the first time since his arrival, dressed formally in a dark-blue suit, white shirt, and tie, he simply stated, Errands.

On Saturday, as on the days prior, he awaited me in his room. He lay fully clothed on his bed, smoking. Mild air blew in through the open window, but his icy expression suggested a sudden drop in temperature, perhaps triggered by a phone call from Wanda. His gaze searched my face as if I were a stranger. He told me to get undressed, but there was no hunger in the way he watched. He was squinting, his lips open just enough to let the smoke escape. I didn't know if he was studying my movements or inspecting my figure or pondering something else related to my body.

What is it? I asked. And when he didn't answer, but just kept smoking, I asked again, What is it?

Your voice is nice, he said. Too nice, or can you say, dangerously nice?

I didn't understand. I thought, Love will solve this. But it didn't solve a thing. Our bodies collided, a perfect fit no longer.

His express letter from Monte Carlo reached me on April 20, of all days, the Führer's fiftieth birthday.

Your psychiatrist . . . forbids you from having a sexual relationship with me.

There it was. He had visited the psychiatrist's office in the

Bellevue building Friday afternoon, despite having refused to do so in the past. Volodya's handwriting was more tangled than ever. I had to reread it three times to decipher what he was telling me. The doctor, who considered himself my doctor and was paid by my father, didn't forbid Horowitz from sleeping with me for my sake, but for his. Because I was supposedly using him for sex, using sex for entrapment. I knew exactly what I was doing, getting him to need me in this way, the doctor had said, but my passion was put on. It had nothing to do with love, which was why I was always cavorting with others. I'd only stopped sleeping with women because I was stingy and couldn't be bothered with the rigmarole of flowers, outings, and perfumes. That, Horowitz scribbled, was apparently what I had told my psychiatrist myself!

The things he wrote were like his handwriting—tangled. He had always idealized me, and still did, he wrote, but I had sullied his love and ideals with my duplicity, and . . . Hang on, I need the original.

Kaufmann searched for the letter. You have to understand that unless I read it aloud, I can't get the words out, even half a century later. Here it is.

That's the very type of person I hate, hate, and hate!!! Three exclamation points. *Yet I still write, because I am thinking this could be a medical maneuver. . . . One of you two is like a criminal targeting me! I am very upset . . . And now I'm the one going crazy, but then it's over, 100% . . . Still yours, Volodya.*

You can imagine the state I was in after reading this. Perfect conditions for composing some senseless reply.

There was no time to cool off. He was booked aboard the *SS Normandy* for New York on April 29, leaving Paris the twenty-sixth. How dare *anyone* write me a letter like that, I fumed, Horowitz or not! It was bound to turn out poorly.

Volodya's response was dated April 23, 1939. He must have written it directly upon receiving my mail. I sensed something was amiss, because it opened with *Dear Herr Nico.* And it didn't end there. He said my words provided proof that I was a nobody, far too insignificant to concern the likes of a Horowitz. And in his last letter, in which he'd put all his cards on the table, he was simply fulfilling his responsibility to me as the older and more respectable of us two. Then he unleashed a tirade about my psychiatrist; the entire profession was known for making healthy minds sick, after all.

There's nothing like a mutual enemy to bring people together, my grandfather always said. Was this an effort on Volodya's part to exhibit solidarity?

Behind the first page was another, also dated April 23, 1939. The focus there was pianistic.

Should my playing ever come to express something important, he found it only natural—despite his modesty—that his influence might be detected there. Then he drew up recommendations for a concert program. It seemed symbolic, but everything had the potential for symbolism back then.

Beethoven's *Les Adieux* sonata made the list, as did the Brahms *Handel Variations* and various pieces by Chopin. Taking leave, but continuing to play Brahms and Chopin, preserving his influence in my mind and fingers.

Behind that was a third page, but folded up smaller and also dated April 23. That one I have to read to you.

My darling Nico, I know I mustn't write what I'm about to, because you will directly sense your "power" and think, "Nabbed him again!"... but I am always honest and write what I feel!... I wanted to tell you that those three days in Zurich made me love you again.

Whether mental or physical—I love everything about you and from you! Do not think that you are <u>especially</u> beautiful or <u>especially</u> intelligent... but altogether, everything fits and takes on a peculiar nuance that I could call love! But I am tired of seeing you so rarely! You write that you're always with me, even when I'm far away... but now that is hard for me. I am 34 years old...

Kaufmann cleared his throat. He was turning thirty-six that year.

... the best age to enjoy many new experiences. Besides, my temperament is such that when I'm alone, as I am now, and I think of you and see you before me, I am forced to find satisfaction somehow and somewhere... but... what can I do. You're always so far away!

I would remain that way indefinitely. Things didn't look good for the planned summer vacation in Gstaad. Wanda had decided she and Horowitz would stay in the U.S. during that time.

Volodya wrote once more, amid packed suitcases. *Night of April 25th to 26th* was written at the top, and the letter began differently than all the others, with *Dear Nikishin!* Would I please tear up his awful letter. He had underlined that ten times. He apologized for his abusive manner, but he'd had every right to go crazy, if I really thought about it: for someone to take such an emotionally loaded trip, only to learn from a third party that his lover lies through his teeth. . . !

And now, for your favorite topic, Kaufmann said. Guilt and atonement. *I've cried for two days straight, I feel so guilty,* Volodya continued. He had sought sexual release, enlisting one of the Toscaninis' oldest family friends for help, no less, and his conscience now tormented him. *I feel morally like a criminal because of my deep and earnest, real feelings for you! And our real happiness will come when you start to feel the same every time you stray.*

The letter is much longer, but I won't subject you to the whole thing. Horowitz links the question of living morally to that of artistry—he was moved by the care I provided my ailing father and thought it an indication that my spoiled, yet essentially sound character might yet recover. Only the good were capable of creating beautiful, great works of art, and the opposite too, he argued.

I felt dizzy and sick to my stomach as I put aside the letter. How could he, of all people, argue that goodness and beauty were by necessity identical? Reports on the Degenerate Art exhibition in Munich the year before had appeared in our newspapers too, some including non-degenerate examples, like Ziegler, that painter of pubes Hitler so revered, and all manner of blood-and-soil artists. That shoddy output claimed to be beautiful and morally good, just like its creators, and just like Horowitz was suggesting. I had the poems of François Villon on my desk at the time, the ones Brecht had drawn upon for the *Threepenny Opera*. Breathtaking fireworks penned by a hardened criminal. We had read Goethe's *Cellini* in school; he was a sculptor of heroes and holy men who I knew had several murders on his conscience. The sheet music for Gesualdo da Venosa's madrigals, pieces that plumb human depths, was on my shelf. The composer was a murderer, twice over. A few feet over were the Debussy renderings of poems by Verlaine, who had shot and killed his former lover, Rimbaud. I was aware that one of my favorite painters, Caravaggio, was also a slayer, and . . . all right, enough. Criminality and remorselessness are not prerequisites for making art, but sometimes art is created by the criminal and remorseless, plain and simple. That's true to this day.

Kaufmann approached the bookcase, climbed the stepladder, pulled a volume from an upper shelf to the left, and opened it. *Philosophy for Non-Philosophers*, I read it just a few years ago, when the author, Louis Althusser, made headlines for strangling his wife. I wrote down one of his lines on the endpapers: *To philosophize with open eyes is to philosophize in the dark. Only the blind can look straight at the sun.*

He stepped off the ladder and moved a chair to sit facing Donati with his back to the piano.

I careened through the city for the rest of the day and all night, didn't eat, drank too much, then did exactly what Horowitz was expecting: I sent a photo of myself express, one taken in the summer after a swim, where my lips were barely parted and you could clearly see my incisors—he loved my lips and my incisors—to provide a basis for . . . let's call them daydreams. I would do whatever humanly possible to make moral improvements, I wrote, to grow closer to him. I took it very seriously, I told him.

Donati straightened in his chair. Did you?

XIII

❧⸱❧

Zurich, Kaufmann had often explained to visitors, wasn't the kind of city where people showed emotion in their faces. The sight of couples was reminder enough that there was no Swiss expression for *I love you*, let alone a future tense. Whenever spring finally consented to becoming spring-like, the occasional passerby might be caught smiling to himself in satisfaction, but Kaufmann couldn't recall ever having witnessed a Zurich local grin in public.

Horowitz à Moscou. It had made the front page of a couple French newspapers, while a photo of Horowitz in an elegant coat with hat and cane, grinning after landing at Sheremetyevo Airport, graced the cover of two magazines and an arts journal. You'll have to explain why he's grinning like that, Donati said.

He bought every publication featuring Horowitz, set the pile on the nearest car roof, and, despite the drizzle, stood there and began tearing through the pages with a voracity Kaufmann would never have expected of him.

What's gotten into you?

Of all people to ask such a thing, Donati answered. A week ago, I was indifferent to him. Do you have cable?

I don't even own a television, Kaufmann said with the air of a Michelin-starred chef asked for a side of ketchup.

Donati tore out a page, folded it to the size of a postcard, and stuffed it into the inside pocket of his coat. Then he gathered the remaining papers into a sloppy pile and clamped them under his arm. A new station called 3sat is airing the concert, which the Americans are recording, in Germany, Austria, and Switzerland. Horowitz is playing in the Great Hall of the Moscow Conservatory in the afternoon, then the recording will be broadcast here later.

When is he playing?

Starting at four p.m.

He has performed at four in the afternoon for I don't know how many years! What day?

Tomorrow.

April 20?

April 20.

It just had to be on the Führer's birthday, and in Moscow, at that!

Your diagnosis clearly holds up, Donati said. Politics don't interest him.

They left the newspaper stand and ambled along the lakeshore, Kaufmann leading the way, Donati following.

Now that he's an American citizen, it seems only fitting he would choose this particular moment to visit Moscow, right after the U.S. imposed a boycott on the Soviet Union for its loyalty to Gaddafi, Donati commented.

He stopped at the first unoccupied bench on the Bürkliterrasse, sat on his newspapers, and began to study the magazine photos. Kaufmann gazed at the lightening gray on the water, while Donati grew incensed.

Have they lost their blessed minds? Special military transport for his grand piano! Lowered with ropes from his living room in New York, flown by jet to Moscow, escorted—as though it were cash-in-transit!—to the American embassy, where they heaved it through the window to his room with a crane, only to remove it yesterday, again under military supervision. And then twenty Russian giants were enlisted to carry it into the conservatory concert hall for the open rehearsal. They even flew in his piano technician! How do they hope to turn a profit? What insanity.

Kaufmann sat with folded hands beside him.

Wise, Kaufmann said, very wise. Volodya would never have agreed otherwise. All soloists—we're talking violinists, cellists, flutists, oboists—they all travel with their own instrument. It's a comfort to have your treasured partner there. You know exactly what turns it on or pisses it off, where it will overreact, and what pushes it to climax. The fact that instruments have bodies says it all. Pianists are constantly shacking up with someone new, who may look like the one at home, but that's about it. Which only makes the sense of abandonment more pronounced.

Donati was not convinced. Oh please, the man needs

his own personal piano tuner? That's as fussy and entitled as his . . . what was it again? Here . . . his demand that they fly in apple juice from Normandy, asparagus from northern Italy, and fresh Dover sole. Asparagus or sole may be hard to come by in Moscow, but there must be a hundred piano tuners.

It would appear you are confusing a Steinway with a car. There's nothing special about the grand piano Horowitz plays, per se, but he could identify it among thousands of pianos by the sound of a single scale. Just as you would recognize your mother's voice among thousands with your eyes closed.

Donati was absorbed in photos of a mustachioed man intently overseeing movers in shirtsleeves liberating the swaddled body of the piano from a wooden crate addressed to Maestro Horowitz.

Doesn't leave much for the tuner to do, though, does it? If his Steinway has such a unique sound.

A reasonable misconception. A good voice is little more than an organ; it takes more than that to be a good singer. Even Steinway has built pianos lacking that internal organ. What becomes of the instrument ultimately depends on the manner in which the pianist plays it—that is, how it feels in his hands, how it comes to life, how much or little force it requires. To produce that effect in foreign surroundings takes the handiwork of a technician whose senses are steeped in that manner of playing. He prepares the piano for the act of love.

Donati turned to Kaufmann, cleared his throat in exasperation, and raised his eyebrows. Kaufmann beamed at him.

After all, it is _der Flügel_ and _le piano_, masculine nouns in both German and French.

Donati was not amused.

What about Wanda? he asked, as if he were her lawyer.

The last line Volodya sent from the steamboat on April 30, 1939, sounded assured of victory: _I am certain, as long as nothing gets in the way, like war or illness, that I will soon be with you again._ Back in Paris in early June, he wrote and apologized for his scrawl. Wanda, who had strictly forbidden him from making contact or exchanging letters with me, continually got in the way. I found it reckless of him to keep inviting me to Paris or Bagnoles de l'Orne. Wanda would surely discover who was cavorting with her husband in her absence. Volodya saw my point and made long-term plans. Starting in October or November, I should join him on tour.

What? On the road with him alone for weeks on end? Donati asked.

It was important for my development as a human and as a musician, Horowitz explained. Then he added, _Don't laugh._ I'll never forget that. Otherwise, he clung to the illusion that time had solved the problem. He insisted I visit him every two weeks at his summer residence in Gstaad, instruction included, and extended the invitation to my parents and sister. We had to meet beforehand, though, to launch a major diplomatic offensive. He wanted to spell out what I should write to Wanda; I would then explain to my father what _he_ should write to her. Volodya was glowing with optimism.

After a few letters, it will be smooth sailing, he claimed. By now I knew what to expect following these highs of his.

On July 2, 1939, I received a long letter from him, sent from a spa where he was taking the cure. It was a letter in three parts: *Your Page / My Page / Our Page.* In the first part, he stated that, should I share the opinion of my parents and shrink, namely that my homosexual activity hinged solely on him, then he never wanted to see me again, because this cast him as the evil tempter, a role he had no interest in accepting. If, however, male love was something I couldn't live without, then I should prove my age of twenty-three and finally get it through my father's head that it would be better to have a gentleman friend like him than multiple men à la carte, as he always put it. In short, I should move out.

I couldn't believe what he wrote next: I mustn't forget his wife loved him madly.

Loved him madly, Donati repeated. Not bad, as far as idioms go. Who was it, Goethe or Shakespeare presumably, who said there's method to his madness.

Yes, method to his and hers. Milstein told me that after the first time Wanda saw him perform solo, she declared, He's the world's best on piano, his look is perfect for a pianist, and he alone is a match for my father's brilliance. I'm going to marry him.

So she actually worshipped him at first? Everything else you've told me was a far cry from worship. What did she call him, anyway? Volodya, Vladimir, Horowitz, or . . .

Pinci. She called him Pinci.

Pinci? Donati leapt to his feet and stared at Kaufmann. Pinci, really? And he put up with that?

Kaufmann responded in bewilderment that Horowitz had spoken as little Italian as he.

Donati sat back down on his newspapers.

Pinci are something I remember from my *nonna*'s kitchen. They're noodles, pale, handmade, and thin, but misshapen, like bungled *spätzle*. One is called a *pincio*, strongly suggestive of *pinco*, or dimwit. I'm sure the Toscaninis were thoroughly amused by that. But excuse me, I interrupted you. Part three?

Our Page opened with the usual accusations. He described my earlier existence as prostituted, something absolutely abhorrent to him. Still, he allowed that if the summer brought us any new clarity, I could come to America with him for five months.

The next double letter from Volodya in early July revealed where things really stood between us. For outward appearances, he wrote something along the lines of, I'm sorry, but I won't act counter to Papa's will. What he wrote to me, though, and I just reread the section yesterday, really got me going: *We will engage in a war of nerves! But adagio! We will win.*

A war of nerves. Chamberlain had been quoted on the radio using those very terms. Horowitz made no mention of the looming world war. He was focused instead on a personal feud and his hope for a musical ceasefire with his father-in-law. Toscanini had called for him to play the

Brahms Piano Concerto No. 2 on August 29 in Lucerne. Brahms! For Volodya it went without saying that I would attend this historic event. Tickets were sold out immediately, and under no circumstances could I let Wanda spot my face. Still, he had a ticket sent to me—gallery, first row, directly above the podium. Wanda and the rest of the clan would be seated below, at the very front, with a clear view of the spectators above.

He giggled on the phone when I expressed my fear. Wanda only has eyes for the famous, he said. She doesn't even register the audience in the cheaper seats.

You're not going, said my father.

On August 23, 1939, the German-Soviet Nonaggression Pact was signed in Moscow. Everyone sensed what that meant. Whoever hoped to make a run for America had better hurry.

You're still not going, said my father.

Three days later, the conscription age in France was extended by three years to include another seven hundred thousand men. My grandfather was beside himself. If the French are planning a flank march through our country, to get involved in Poland, we're done for. My father sent the maid downstairs with valerian, which my grandfather sent right back.

On August 28, I made as much noise as possible rummaging around my mother's dressing room; I hooked a small valise from the top of the wardrobe and left my bedroom door wide open as I packed.

Taking a trip, Herr Nico? the maid asked.

Two minutes later, my father appeared. If you go through with this . . .

I looked him in the eyes. If I don't go through with this . . .

And I closed my suitcase with a snap.

At the train station, the morning papers announced, *Swiss Border Protection Troops Summoned, Federal Assembly Convenes, General Elected.*

The seat cushions in the train were sweating. No one spoke. Many sat clutching their upper arms and staring at the floor.

It was a much different scene at the concert hall in Lucerne; judging from the crowd, not a thing was amiss. The air was thick with self-satisfaction. Their applause as Toscanini approached the podium was already exaggerated, but grew downright hysterical when Horowitz scurried on stage.

To have them both here in Europe; this will be the last time for who knows how long, the woman beside me commented.

The concerto opens with the call of a horn. *Waldeinsamkeit*, I thought. Forest solitude. It was a word Horowitz had discovered somewhere and fallen in love with. The hall couldn't have been quieter if it were empty. It was as if the tension spilled over from Horowitz into the audience. He kept glancing at Toscanini like a nervous debutant.

And then came the third movement, an adagio passage in F sharp . . . No, you'll have to hear it. His back trembled, just his back. I could see his hands from above. They rested there quietly, and his fingers drew tones I had never heard from the keys. Final tones. Toscanini lowered his baton.

All rose to their feet at the end. I studied the faces. They appeared to have aged, as though they had unexpectedly looked death in the eye.

I spent the night in Lucerne by myself, in a coffin-like hotel room. I liked it.

On August 31, I sat on a park bench in Seefeld and read the handful of lines Horowitz had dashed down on Grand Hotel National stationery following the concert. What was my experience of the Brahms? He had poured his soul into it. The word *soul* was written in very large letters. I had never seen nor heard him use the word.

I was eating breakfast alone in my room the next day when the news came over the radio: Germany at war with Poland. Effective immediately, the Free City of Danzig, its territory and citizenry, belonged to the German Reich.

On September 2, I ran onto the street at dawn. Why I headed for my old school, I couldn't tell you. A sign was hung outside the Freies Gymnasium building: *Temporarily closed*. Another sign had been stuck to a wall with an arrow pointing toward the schoolyard. *Assembly area*, it read. Students drifted in with soldiers from out of town, whom they'd escorted from the train station. One of them stopped. Kaufmann? Alumnus? I nodded. Haven't enlisted yet? He spat on the ground. Four hundred thirty thousand men have already been mobilized.

Not a peep from Horowitz, no word, no sign.

My ears were like radio receivers. I listened for the telephone around the clock. No calls for me. On September 3, 1939, Great Britain and France declared war against Germany. The British government annulled all German visas. Visa holders were now considered enemies of the state. Even German Jews were banned from emigrating to Great Britain. Same went for their Russian counterparts.

Sorry, said Donati, but where was Horowitz's passport from?

Kaufmann stood up with some effort. Donati clamped his newspapers under his arm. Without asking where they were going, he followed Kaufmann northward.

You're quicker than I am. That day was the first time I stopped to think about it. What was it I had seen among his things? There was a flimsy-looking document, a greenish scrap, nothing to it, *Passeport de Nansen* printed across the top. That was all I remembered. One of my secondary school classmates had gotten a job with the customs authority. The Nansen passport? It's a makeshift solution that bigshot polar explorer thought up for stateless refugees and emigrants back in '22 when he was Commissioner of the League of Nations. Why do you ask? my old pal wanted to know.

A year earlier, Lenin had decided to revoke the citizenship of all Russian expats. Their papers were now worthless.

Nansen passports are issued by the emigrant's current country of residence, my acquaintance continued. They expire after a year, though. As for U.S. visas? Used to be the passport was good for obtaining one of those, but since the war began, things are looking pretty grim.

The fear buffeted me from all sides, even at home. In our president's unnaturally deepened voice as he urged for prudence and restraint, or from our cook's shopping bags, bulging with jars of lard, packets of butter, bacon, and bottles of oil. It even jumped out of ads in the paper. Virtuous residential architects offered their services in constructing air-raid shelters, while bedroom furniture stores advertised emergency cots with protective mattresses. I couldn't take it anymore on Seefeld Quai. But the entire city was unbearably tense. Panic infused every sound you heard—a horse's whinny, a clatter, a sob, snort, laugh, or commotion. Soldiers were on the move with their knapsacks, and the roads were full of dung; more than seventy thousand horses had been mobilized. Lines for the grocery store extended into the street. Much of the staff had been drafted, they explained, even women, for the army's auxiliary.

I finally received an express letter on September 13, sent the day before from a private residence in Lucerne. *The last two weeks have been so difficult, it's felt like two years!* Volodya wrote. He had called and called, but was always informed I wasn't at home.

Kaufmann and Donati continued in silence, until they reached the Baur au Lac.

Why are we here? Donati asked.

Kaufmann passed wordlessly through the entrance. We

won't need it long, he said, as the toned young man at reception handed him a key with a decorous smile.

It was a large room with a view of the lake. Kaufmann sat on the bed, Donati in the brocade armchair opposite.

I was as sweaty and dusty as a cur that's been trailing a bitch in heat for days. That's how it was too. I had been monitoring the Baur au Lac every day since September 13, keeping an eye on the entrance. Horowitz had reported he was already here, wrapping a few things up—with his wife. She won't turn her back for a second, he had warned. He told me to leave messages for him with a friend at the Schauspielhaus theater. I was on the brink. For Volodya to be so close, for the very last time, and not be able to reach him.

I feverishly woke every morning at four; I was horrified by what I saw in the mirror. The mask of addiction, my father would have called it. When I wasn't sneaking around the hotel, I was at the Schauspielhaus, asking if he'd sent word.

Finally, on September 16, there was a note in a hotel envelope: Wanda had left.

It was this room. The hallways were deserted. No more athletic young men around, or unathletic, for that matter. All had been drafted. Come in, Volodya called. He had locked the door. I jiggled the handle. There was silence, then I heard his voice from up close; he must have been right behind the door. Nikishin? he asked.

I was faced with a spooked animal, pale as a newt that

had crept from a hole in the ground, eyes that had long seen nothing but darkness.

Wanda's perfume still hung in the air.

Bundles of cash were stacked on the desk over there, alongside strongboxes, velvet cases, and coffers. He had emptied some safe or other and wanted me to help him count the dollars and gold coins and pack up his Fabergé cigarette cases. Too few people in the building, Horowitz said. The mobilization.

I had to count up his fortune myself while he sat beside me. He leaned his head back and spoke.

The French consul in Lucerne had sat front and center in the concert hall on August 29. He, too, had risen to his feet in awe of Volodya's Brahms. Three days later, he denied Horowitz's application for an American visa, refusing to accept the French-issued Nansen passport he presented. Horowitz was stopped as he left the consulate—Papers, please—because he was shaking so badly. Wanda had an Italian passport. The words *Toscanini's daughter* were all the Italian consul had to hear. It was no longer a favored title. He harangued them at length, made several long phone calls, and after two hours, merely presented them with travel permits to Genoa. There were staffers in the foreign ministry there, for whom Toscanini was a god and Mussolini a criminal. They finally received their visas for the U.S. and immediately booked the journey from Genoa to New York, by way of Valencia. They got the last spots on the ship. But . . .

Donati leaned in. But what?

Kaufmann had crumpled where he sat and spoke without lifting his head.

I was left waiting for the hunger to set in. Desire in the face of danger wasn't working out the way I'd hoped. I felt castrated. The prudish feel of freshly printed bills between my fingers, the click of the small mechanical calculator I was entering figures into, numbers, nothing but numbers before me. Our last time, maybe our very last time. And there I was, summoned as a stooge to handle the accounting.

He had ultimately reclined beside Horowitz on the mattress wearing nothing but his unbuttoned shirt, and though still trapped in the calculations and thoughts of greed and parsimony and cash, he had waited to see if anything might happen.

Listen, bubele, Horowitz said wearily, I'm not free. But I'm going to America, where more people have bought their freedom than anywhere else on earth. Do you understand?

Then his cool hand reached for mine . . .

What happened between you two that final evening, or final night? Donati asked, catching Kaufmann before his mind drifted.

What's that? You want to know what happened? Nothing, said Kaufmann. We both took it too seriously. It was nothing and everything at once.

He trailed off, lost in thought. As the six o'clock bells rang for vespers, he roused himself.

Once they were back outside, Kaufmann said, He gave me a goodbye present. A rose-gold Cartier wristwatch. It was later stolen from me in a mugging in Munich. His only other gift, the cast-off Lanvin cardigan, fell victim to moths.

Horowitz grinned at them from the next newspaper stand.

Why, though? Donati asked. Why that grin?

It's his last stand. He always loved ice cream. She wouldn't let him have any. I just want what's best for him, she claimed. He loved men, but she drove them away. He loved dancing in nightclubs, but she allowed it only on major birthdays. He grinned a lot—maybe there was part of him that wanted to go off the rails—and she forbade it. But grinning was the one thing she couldn't take away from him.

Kaufmann smiled. And by the look of it, she still can't.

XIV

❦

TRAVELING LIGHT. Sounds carefree, Kaufmann thought as he stuffed sweets into a small paper bag at the candy shop.

One pair of underpants (white), one pair of socks (anthracite), one shirt (light blue), and a toothbrush. He whistled to himself, but only recognized the tune once he reached a dead end. *Voyager sans bagages*, a song for voice and piano; he had begun composing it in late 1939, but never gotten past the first draft.

Late 1939. Many of the artists with a red *J* in their passports, who cycled through the Odeon that fall, or even later, to scrounge up the cash they needed for smugglers to help them escape through France and the Pyrenees to Spain, in the hopes of catching the last steamboat from Valencia, were never heard from again. Traveling light.

The human drama contained within those two words, Kaufmann murmured.

Which two? asked Donati.

Oh, nothing.

On the way from Kreis 4 to the lake—to cable television in

Meilen—Kaufmann asked Donati to make a brief stop in the old city center, at the Hotel Hirschen in Niederdorf.

It was a narrow building, whose dignity in old age was smothered by a coat of salmon-pink paint. The thud of distorted drumming issued from the first floor: lots of noise, little else.

Donati grimaced. When I was twenty-four, I saw Pink Floyd live for the first time at Hirschenbühne. This was a happening place back in '69.

Isn't it wonderful? Kaufmann was beaming. Youth is a condition that clears up without any treatment required. Thirty-five years ago, when I still suffered its effects, there was a man from eastern Switzerland by the name of Carigiet, Zarli Carigiet, who installed two enormous green plywood pickles to the right and left of this door. From 1934 onward, following a false start, the Cabaret Cornichon became an institution. Guests clustered on hard stools around tray-sized tables and passed down the small bottles of wine or plates of stale sandwiches served by battle-hardened waitresses. After the war started, the Cornichon became a primary focus of the German embassy's counselor in Bern, a man by the name of von Bibra. He could barely keep up with his own injunctions against this pigsty. With all the letters they received, the Cornichon could have papered the walls five times over. Starting in the fall of 1940, this became my home as a pianist.

The moment Kaufmann said the word *home*, he felt a wistful pang as he recalled the smell of that stale, steamy old den.

Donati gazed at his profile sympathetically. Seems the trauma of Horowitz leaving threw you off course pretty damn quick.

Nice of you to think that, but in the fall of 1940, I received my diploma in performance from the Zurich Conservatory. I wanted to rub it in my old teacher's face. *You could be a decent pianist, but as far as a career is concerned, I remain skeptical!* Volodya had made sure to point out in one of his final letters.

I sat listening to the radio at six in the morning on April 19, 1941. I had placed a photo on top of it that Volodya had given me upon his departure: *To my dear Nico, in remembrance of his teacher, who regrets the disruption of studies due to unfortunate circumstances.*

The concert was broadcast directly to our island from Carnegie Hall, Horowitz and Toscanini performing Tchaikovsky. It was a miracle to me. Since my twenty-fourth birthday on June 24, 1940, Switzerland had been surrounded by the Axis Powers. Wheat, cabbage, and carrots were being grown in town squares, private gardens, and parks. Oh, excuse me, why am I telling *you* that? . . . It was the first form of contact I'd had with Volodya in a year and a half. Things must have been going well over there; he was in top form. After he finished, the radio vibrated for minutes on end with a sound like pouring rain, which said it all. New Yorkers were celebrating, something music could accomplish in times of darkness.

Donati appeared unmoved. Or maybe it was the triumph of having Toscanini and Horowitz in their custody they were celebrating. As for you, if you had such lofty goals, what were you doing at the Hirschen, slumming it with the beer and sausage and revue performers? I'd imagine they were dilettantes, the whole lot.

Without saying a thing, Kaufmann got in the passenger side of the old Peugeot and simply sat there, fiddling with his cuff links until the car left the city and hugged the right side of the lake, headed south.

His name was Carlo, at least that's what he was called at the Cornichon; to the outside world, he was Karl Meier. Illegitimate son of a laundry worker, almost twenty years my senior, primary school education followed by training to become a salesman—nothing proper, my father would have said. Nevertheless, he had accomplished his dream of becoming an actor and director—they'd offered him the position as theater director in Schaffhausen. And he was openly gay.

He wasn't much to look at, with slightly bulbous, sad eyes and a weedy frame. Unmusical too. And then there were those who knew him as Rolf. That was the name he used as publisher of the magazine *Human Right*, the predecessor to *The Circle*. Rolf also headed an association of gay men and organized their galas. Guests would travel from across Europe and transform from drab suit-and-tie caterpillars into dazzling butterflies. It was . . .

Yes? Donati urged.

It was all such a lie. Theoretically speaking, as of 1942, the human rights of homosexuals were officially protected in Switzerland, but in practice, gays were forced out of jobs and homes and disowned by their families if the truth came to light. I would prefer you had cancer—that would at least spare us the disgrace, the father of Rolf's treasurer had told his son as he kicked him out.

Rolf the devout, who had spent his childhood in prayer, came this close to hanging himself as a boy, because he believed his orientation to be a deadly sin. Since admitting the truth to himself, he saw no reason to beat around the bush, and the same went for me. Bisexual? I think you just claim that for your parents' sake, so they'll think you can be converted.

We buried my father in 1942, and I realized Rolf was right. I told my mother.

Where did the courage suddenly come from? Donati asked.

I never rose to any great acts of courage. That Jewish medical student in Davos in 1936? You know, the one who simply strolled into Wilhelm Gustloff's home, the head of the Swiss Nazi party, and shot him point-blank? He was only a few years older than me. I would never have dared do such a thing. At the very least, I wanted to be big enough for the lesser acts of courage. I felt compelled to send a card to Volodya: I never became normal, and I won't be getting married. Yours, Nikishin. But to me, he was no more than a figure on the radio or at the newsstand now.

Rachmaninoff Dead at 70 in Los Angeles After Long Serious Illness. The headline reached us in late March of 1943. His friend Horowitz, I read, had relocated to Los Angeles with his wife and daughter and since cancelled all upcoming concerts, save one with Toscanini. It seemed the fear of the maestro remained.

In May of 1943, I would have loved to send Volodya a telegraph reading, *won scholarship competition in piano. prize restricted to use for further study.* Work! Work! Work! Volodya had impressed upon me, although he rarely practiced himself.

I don't know if it was vanity or sentimentality or maybe even genuine need that made me hope for a sign of life from Volodya after the war.

. . . who regrets the disruption of studies was written on the picture. Even back then, every newsstand carried magazines and newspapers in ten different languages. It was an art magazine that ran a sort of human interest story about Horowitz in December of 1945. He posed with Sonia and Wanda on the sofa under a Picasso. The caption read, *The star pianist sold his collection of Fabergé and purchased a townhouse on 94th Street in New York, near Central Park.*

Did he happen to recall who had packed up all those Fabergé cigarette cases for him? I came close to shelling out my recent windfall on a flight to New York. I had just won the first prize for piano in the Concours de Genève, at age twenty-nine. Georg Solti had won it three years earlier, and Arturo Benedetti Michelangeli three years before that. Friedrich Gulda would win it the following year. . . I know those names don't mean much to you. Think of Michelangeli as your Jimi Hendrix, Gulda as your Frank Zappa. But Volodya would have understood. Then I studied the photo. It was terrifying.

Donati waited.

He waited in vain.

The engine of the old Peugeot provided the only sound.

Kaufmann finally stirred as they approached Erlenbach. *Medi, my God. Of all moments for us to drive past the Manns' again. I saw Medi Mann in Chicago in the spring of 1947.*

Donati hit the brakes. *What? You performed in Chicago?*

Indeed, but at their equivalent of the Hirschen. Horowitz had proven right; I never did make it as a pianist, at least not one he'd have recognized as such, although things briefly had appeared to be headed that way. It was for the best.

What do you mean, it was for the best? Donati's voice had grown unusually loud.

Just that. A true artist has an inner drive, whereas I require it from outside sources. There was no one left for me to prove myself to. No father, no Horowitz, not even a lover to impress. The Cornichon had closed, and I was touring the U.S. with one of the cabaret's former stars, dancer and panto-mime artist Trudi Schoop. Our piece was called Barbara, *set to a ballet score I'd composed. I kept Volodya's very last letter to me, written hastily from Valencia on October 1, 1939, in the inside pocket of my jacket, behind my passport, as if it were my second form of identification. There were two lines he'd written that were like a . . . like a promise to me. It was . . . such luck that we could be together again before my departure! . . . It was truly fated.*

In Detroit I read in the newspaper that Horowitz was also touring the States, performing that day, I believe, in

Boston. Since he always went to the venue around noon to position his Steinway and test the acoustics, I tried reaching him there. It worked. I was aroused by the sound of his voice after all those years. He was too. It was like we were tearing our clothes off over the phone as we feverishly confessed our concerns and dreams and desires to one another.

Where did things stand with my father, he wanted to know, and with my lovers?

He died a slow, miserable death, and it was at his grave-side that I finally realized where I truly belonged, sexually.

What about my living situation, my finances?

Sadly still at home in Seefeld, no way around it, yes, pretty strapped for cash, but I was getting by.

Wanda?

Says I'm fine on piano but good for nothing as a human. She even says it in front of other people.

Sonia?

Totally out of control. Paints pictures, gets expelled from every school, steals, lies, and has a filthy mouth. She's no longer my child.

Rachmaninoff's death?

It was terrible. We won't see each other again, Volodya, he said to me shortly before he died. He believed in nothing, and now neither do I, except for . . . Volodya's voice broke off.

I stood in the phone booth at my hotel. I had placed the Cartier watch from Volodya on the wooden console. Barely fifteen minutes had passed, yet we had asked everything of each other.

Please write me a long, detailed letter, he begged me hoarsely. You have no idea how alone I am. I need your . . . I heard noise in the background on the other end of the line, first a man speaking, then a woman, loud, then louder. Volodya hung up without saying goodbye.

I wrote him a long, detailed letter. I didn't mention my honky-tonk tour. I just told him I was now successful and up for anything, maybe even in the States, then suggested two or three places we could meet. I finally received a response in Chicago, delivered by his agent, Sol Hurok. I knew from the papers that Hurok's real name was Solomon Izrailevich Gurkow. Jewish and Russian. Vladimir Samoylovich Gorowiz was clearly yearning for some sense of home in that foreign land. Wanda and Sonia provided it as little for him as he presumably did for them. Could I be the one to provide it? I tore open the envelope with my index finger; my finger was trembling. The letter started out well. Horowitz was happy to hear of my achievements, very happy. The letter was brief. It closed with the line, *It's better if we never see each other again.*

I was headed for lunch at Medi's when I read those words. She had married a Sicilian intellectual named Borgese, thirty-six years her senior—yes, you're thinking what everyone thought. Staunch antifascist since youth, now an environmental activist and university professor, to boot.

I thought I might throw up in the elevator.

My father calls him Vulcan, Medi breathed in my ear as Borgese shook my hand. He looked to me like an elderly François Villon might have. Thick, unusually red lips for a man, bulging nose, wide nostrils, lecherous eyes. Though they didn't have much money, they did have an imposing apartment in Chicago with a view of Lake Michigan, a black maid, and two young daughters, ages seven and three. Medi was comforted to hear I'd abandoned my career as a pianist. She had once nurtured the same dream, but had given it up eight years earlier, following the wedding, she explained. Cleared it out like a weed was how she put it.

I suspect it was the husband, Donati said. Vulcan.

No, not at all. We discovered we had both jumped ship for the same reason: we didn't need it to survive. We were pianists, but we weren't artists. Art is born of necessity, Schoenberg said. We were both more than happy not practicing—happier, in fact.

Medi knew Horowitz had taken me on as a student for two years, knew I'd even had lessons in his hotel room when he was vacationing. She envied that, but otherwise knew nothing about us. In her eyes, I was still a handsome boy who would have married her on the spot—a very handsome boy, in fact, according to her father. But it didn't escape her that I was jittery and distracted, and I would imagine my smile was pretty forced. My cheery mood was like brushwood laid over a pitfall. I was close to tears as I showed the Borgeses Volodya's letter. Medi's husband was outraged. He thought it shameful of Horowitz to rebuff me in this manner, without providing any reasons. He was ready to write to Horowitz himself. Then Medi pulled out several articles she had clipped over the past two years.

He goes by Janis, Byron Janis, but his real name is Jankelevich, of Russian Jewish extraction, Medi told me.

Standing with Volodya in every photo was a boy in a black suit, whom Leonardo would have insisted on painting in the nude.

Star Pianist Horowitz Takes on First Student

Byron Janis (16) to Become First-ever Student of Horowitz

Virtuoso as Pedagogue: Horowitz Accepting Students for First Time Ever

I tore up his letter, opened a window, and released the scraps into the wind.

You're free of him now, Medi said.

The following day, I came across a poster announcing, *Horowitz Carnegie Hall N.Y. on May 19, 1947.* I tried to get my hands on a ticket to the sold-out performance through his agent. Utterly impossible, he said. Regardless, I caught the very next train to New York. A friend of mine, Gordon Manley, a pianist from Vancouver, had connections among the door staff and snuck me in for free.

Horowitz played Chopin and Liszt, that much I remember, but I was so dazed I've forgotten most of the details. There's one thing I'll never forget, though. Volodya performed part of the *Années de pèlerinage*, a piano cycle in which Liszt dedicates his own years of pilgrimage to specific countries; the suite Volodya played was from the first year, *Suisse*. A long, homesick lament sung on the keys. Was it his homesickness, or mine, or ours? Was it me he was looking for when he stood and searched the crowd, his hand shading his eyes?

Come backstage and say hello, Gordon urged me. I didn't want to risk the humiliation of Volodya brushing me off, but I did want to see him up close. I ducked into an unlit corner. As he descended the short staircase from the stage, headed for the green room, he folded his hands across his chest, something he'd never done in the past; it was a godfatherly pose Toscanini was known for. He appeared harried and joyless. His face and neck muscles twitched, his skin was pallid, his gait sluggish. Maestro, I heard. Maestro, it was fabulous. That's the accepted form of address now for his inner circle, Gordon whispered. Picked it up from his father-in-law.

Over a beer afterward, Gordon dished up stories, both firsthand and things he'd heard. Volodya's piano technician had to unload periodically on his pal Gordon Manley when the going got tough. He told Gordon that Horowitz had thrown a water glass at him because it wasn't clean. And that he sometimes pounded the keys with his fists and pummeled the lid prop until the lid came crashing down. And that his green room was now wordlessly furnished with a cot, because he wore himself ragged with violent tantrums before every performance. I'm starting to think there's something Horowitz hates about himself, Gordon said.

It suddenly clicked in my mind. Love is born of necessity. Did Horowitz hate himself for not loving as he needed to love? If that was the case, I now understood why Volodya could never see me again: I reminded him that he had chosen to live a lie. I was his conscience.

About six years later, Gordon came to Seefeld for a visit. Criminally good, he said, as he handed over his gift, a bootleg recording of the January 12, 1953 Carnegie Hall performance. Honoring the twenty-fifth anniversary of his first concert there, Horowitz played the Tchaikovsky piano concerto, naturally. He'd selected Dimitri Mitropoulos as conductor. Mitropoulos got sick. George Szell stepped in.

That terrorist can set whatever tempo he wants, Horowitz had told his piano technician, but I'm sticking to mine.

Gordon simply said, And that's exactly what he did. Take a listen.

Horowitz played as though he were fleeing something, and his virtuosity had tacked wings on his heels. In the finale, he overshot the mark, sending chords crashing fortissimo to either side of the beat and crossing the finish line noticeably sooner than the orchestra.

The audience roared. The pianist was the clear winner among the crowd. Szell had aimed to please. Horowitz overpowered.

Donati slowed the car abruptly. Really? He botched it, yet they cheered? That's unbelievable!

It's human. Surely you've heard about virtuosos selling their soul to the devil. The image says it all. There's something fishy going on here! we clamor. He's possessed, we mustn't fall into his clutches. Yet we do. Maybe that's why music critics love harping on hollow virtuosity, but it's only as hollow or full as the virtuoso's mind. Volodya once said, Those who want to become more than a virtuoso should work on becoming one in the first place. No, it wasn't their cheering that surprised me.

What was it, then?

That he hightailed it. He'd never done that in this concerto, not even under Toscanini.

What was he scared of? I asked Gordon.

He shrugged.

He had a pretty good sense, though, of what had happened over the last six years. The anonymity of big cities, Gordon said, favors the poor and the dull. Everyone else can bank on human indiscretion running without a hitch. It takes two or, at the very most, three stops along the way for information to reach the one place it shouldn't. For years, Volodya had undergone regular electroshock therapy for his depression, without any sign of improvement. He then started seeing a psychiatrist by the name of Kubie, who specialized in making homosexuals normal, as people said back then—Kubie, on the other hand, called it healing. I suspect Wanda had pressured him into it. Kubie endorsed the notion that homosexuals were prone to depression because of the guilt occasioned by their perversion. Justified guilt, Kubie argued. Disguised as an assistant, Gordon had accompanied Volodya's piano technician to the Horowitz residence a few times. There he saw the grand piano that Steinway &

Sons had given Horowitz as a belated wedding gift, of all things. He loved that piano more than anything, they said. Kaufmann laughed bitterly.

Three stories, one for company, one for Wanda, one for Volodya. Nevertheless, husband and wife clashed constantly. Neighbors had issued a joint complaint against the Horowitz-Toscanini household. The famous couple's quarrels could be heard from the street. The first time Gordon visited, Horowitz was in his pajamas, lying on a floral sofa next to the piano as the guests approached. Wanda was ready for them—perfectly painted, coiffed, and cloaked—and extended her hand for their kiss. If she had just one wish, she said, it would be to sell the sofa along with her husband.

Sometimes her one wish is to burn it, the technician divulged in the elevator going down. And she likes quoting Rubinstein, who, though he still considers himself Volodya's friend, openly states that Horowitz as a person is a curious blend of arrogance and stupidity.

Not two years after I spied on Volodya backstage, he moved out of the 94th Street apartment and took up residence in a luxury hotel elsewhere in the city. Kubie appointed his own brother-in-law—a dry drunk and former banker in his mid-fifties—as Volodya's girl Friday. He handled his finances, neuroses, appointments, pills, contracts, hypochondria, everything.

Everything, everything? Donati asked.

Kubie's brother-in-law was a ladies' man, if that's what you mean, and Gordon was certain of it. The guy served as lock and key. In 1950 Gordon came across a big ad run in all the New York City papers: *World-Famous Pianist Seeks Secretary and Personal Travel Assistant. Above Average Pay.*

Obviously it's him, the piano technician confirmed. He warned everyone against applying. Still, Horowitz filled the position in no time, and Gordon immediately recognized the man in his mid-twenties at Horowitz's side. His name was Kenneth Leedom, a failed actor who nevertheless dominated the gay scene from New York to Hollywood, a handsome, fit fellow with good humor and charm to spare.

Donati stopped at the gate to his travertine bunker, but didn't get out. Kaufmann glanced at the residence, uncomprehending and ill at ease, as if it were a medical testing facility.

When Gordon came to visit me in Seefeld in '53, the latest was that Leedom had remained faithful to Volodya, professionally at least, and become indispensable since the sudden death of Kubie's brother-in-law two years earlier. Leedom turned to his friends, a group that included Gordon, to blow off steam.

Volodya could be as sweet and mischievous as a child, then morph into a tyrant and send everyone scrambling for cover. It was not uncommon for him to grab a corner of the tablecloth at mealtimes and yank it to the floor with a crash. Leedom was along for the ride and even permitted to put his bare arm around Volodya's shoulders at George Cukor's notorious parties in L.A. Still, Horowitz was in a bad place.

The critiques went from damaging to devastating. He was a master of musical distortion and exaggeration whose sole objective was to confound his audience, Virgil Thomson, the most prominent of the critics, castigated him. And although Horowitz's playing came across as thrilling, he added, it was monotonous and usually wrong.

Gordon thought Horowitz was buckling under the strain of his double life. He continued to hide his sexual orientation from the outside world. He had moved back in with Wanda and, though not yet fifty, suggested he might retire from the stage. Seemed confident enough . . . but then came an act of desperation . . . You have to unlock the gate, or do you want to give me the key?

XV

❧

WE SHOULD STOP talking about him, Kaufmann said as he opened the car door, or we'll have trouble listening to him later.

You're right, Donati agreed. We should stop.

They then stood by the vehicle, one to the right, one to the left, and looked down at the house and the water.

The lake sprawled out, motionless, and tender green leaves adorned the trees along the banks. It was dry and not exactly bright. The cloud cover hung above them, fixed and impenetrable.

The two men waited without knowing what for. There was a soft breeze. The young shoots and leaves stirred gently, and the lake shimmered in the evening light of spring. Neither could look away.

My mother brought me along on the one pilgrimage she ever took, Donati said, to Einsiedeln Abbey. I was maybe ten. She prayed to the Black Madonna for more than an hour. She was kneeling, while I sat in the pew. Suddenly she turned to me. She's smiling, she said. Do you see her smile? I didn't.

But now I understand what she meant.

Kaufmann and Donati gratefully drew in the air, as if

their sense of smell were improved by the light. Then they started for the door.

The fuzzy gray victim was discovered with a brownish trail of dried blood by its head, caught in a mousetrap right beside the door. Donati's back stiffened. He lowered his key, kicked the trap out of the way, and struggled for breath.

The wheezing didn't subside until he was settled in front of the television with Kaufmann. Each had a plaid throw over his knees and a glass of red, and they stared at the massive, dark screen, the latest and best model. The gulp and whir of the radiator was the only sound. The grandfather clock chimed. Donati had wound it the moment they arrived.

The act of desperation, he said. Please explain.

I thought we were going to stop talking about him, Kaufmann said, but fine. This is your house, after all. New York is a tiny village, Gordon insisted at the time. You couldn't find a Swiss farm town where word gets around quicker. Gordon's landlady's sister worked for management at a private mental hospital—the very one Horowitz had been admitted to. It was called aversion therapy, something invented by behavioral therapists. Their tenet: every undesirable behavior is learned and can therefore be unlearned or, shall we say, systematically drilled out of patients. Aversion therapy is based on the principle of conditioning. Alcoholics, junkies of all stripes, bulimics, anorexics, and those known as sexual deviants . . .

Cut to the chase, please, Donati said. We have to be in Moscow in half an hour.

Kaufmann got up and walked toward the front door. He promptly returned and dropped the dead mouse into Donati's wine.

Donati shrieked.

Kaufmann sat back down. That's the version for alcoholics, a practice dating back to antiquity. Halfway through our current century, more modern methods were employed. One of the members of the Circle unfortunately knew that all too well. The machine was called the *Konvulsator* and was made in Germany—that's right, to top it all off—by Siemens. The patient . . . the *patient*? Anyway, as I was saying, the patient was hooked up to the Konvulsator, then shown pictures of naked men accompanied by an electric shock. Images of naked women were presented shock-free.

Why would Horowitz do that to himself? Donati asked in a strangled voice.

Kaufmann reached for the wine containing the mouse, asked where the bathroom was, and came back with the empty, freshly washed glass.

You couldn't possibly expect . . . Donati jumped to his feet.

He returned with a glass of water and sank into his seat. Why? he huffed. Tell me, why?

Seems he preferred it to questions about his childhood or couples therapy with Wanda. Maybe he thought it assured quicker success. At any rate, he wanted to purge himself of what psychiatrists identified as the reason for his depression. And what Wanda identified as one of his many flaws and what most Americans identified as an illness. The World Health Organization considers it one to this day, and it's 1986; homosexuality is listed in its official manual under ICD code 3020, should you care to look it up.

In 1957, I read in the paper that Mitropoulos had been removed from his post as music director of the New York Philharmonic. Leadership issues were the reason cited, but news of the power struggles and intrigue within the organization traveled all the way to Zurich; those in the know referred to the orchestra as Murder Incorporated. My friend Rolf at the Circle scoffed, Oh please, it's obviously because he's gay. Mitropoulos was never the most circumspect.

Volodya hadn't set foot on stage since 1953. He disregarded all speculation about the motives behind his retreat.

The grandfather clock chimed.

Moscow calls, I know, said Kaufmann. Just one last thing: Volodya's hold on me never lessened, even during the hiatus. If a new recording of his was released, I was the first in Zurich to buy it. And then that comeback of his twelve years later in May of 1965. It was broadcast live from Carnegie Hall. The concert opened with Busoni's transcription of Bach's Toccata, Adagio and Fugue in C Major. The same piece he'd supposedly whipped out to warm up for his final exams in Kiev more than forty years earlier. It was deeply ingrained in him, a safe . . .

Moscow, let's not forget about Moscow, Donati groaned.

Volodya slipped up in the very first measure, and I startled as if at thunder. I later cried as he played the final notes of Schumann's celebrated Fantasie and the silence in Carnegie

Hall flowed out of my radio, broad as the River Limmat. No, he refused to let me go. I cursed at his photo when I received a letter from Gordon in January of 1970 that included a newspaper clipping, I think from the *New York Times*, that read, *Sonia Horowitz (40) Died in Italy by Suicide.* And it troubled me to read that he raked in forty-five thousand dollars per performance, and ten times that for the broadcast of Rachmaninoff's Third. I find there's a certain desperation to greed. About four years earlier, I was at the dentist when I stumbled over a long article about Horowitz in a copy of *Der Spiegel.* He was quoted at the end as saying, *There are three kinds of pianists: Jewish pianists, homosexual pianists, and bad pianists.* The journalist had the final word: *Horowitz is neither gay nor bad.* That troubled me even more.

In 1983, I heard he would be performing in Tokyo for the first time in his life. The tabloids couldn't get enough: the piano god demanded tributes, they wrote. Luxury limo around the clock. Twelve-thousand-dollar-a-night suite in which he'd demanded the hotel install a kitchen, but because that presented issues with recently introduced fire codes, new wallpaper and floors had also had to be put in. Horowitz's fee, including television rights, was allegedly seven figures. Directly following the concert, every last outlet gleefully toppled the idol. A broken old man. The remnants of a deity. A washed-up star trying to milk his own former greatness for profit. I studied every picture I could get my hands on with a magnifying glass. Volodya was at the end of his rope, physically and emotionally. A grotesque grimace on his face, figure gone to seed,

LEA SINGER

gestures awkward, gut spilling over his belt. In some shots, he
appeared in the throes of dementia. Wanda flew after him, and
with good reason. Leedom had quit in 1955 and lived happily
ever after with a man of the theater, Gordon had informed me.
He'd been dead a long time, died young, yet I still recalled our
conversation about the use of medication to treat depression.
Better than electroshock, I figured, but then the way Gordon
described the side effects of the psychotropic drugs, tranquiliz-
ers, and mood enhancers so popular in America . . .

Donati tapped his feet. You're beating around the bush.
Surely Horowitz played in Europe again. When and where
did you last see him?

Less than six months ago, in November of '85, at La
Scala in Milan. I had written to him two years earlier, for
his eightieth birthday. No response. And what then emerged
about him and Wanda in connection with his birthday. . .

Kaufmann observed Donati's feet and swallowed what
was on the tip of his tongue.

To Kaufmann, almost every article had read like a report
on trench warfare from 1917: two armies facing off across an
open field, waiting to watch the carnage unfold. But what
governing forces had sent Wanda and Volodya into battle
and still drove them in their old age? Kaufmann stared at the
black screen, and it stared right back.

So, no word from Horowitz. Nevertheless, you went to
Milan. What were you hoping would happen?

Kaufmann gulped and gulped and gulped until his glass
of red wine was empty.

Moscow, again, let's not forget about Moscow, Donati reminded him.

In short, I'm at an age where you need to guard against sentimentality. What kills you is the increased yearning for touch. Touch moves you, or moves something, which comes as a relief when you fear you've turned to stone.

It was hard to get a ticket, only possible with VIP connections. Mine had been promised to Puccini's granddaughter and cost an arm and a leg. He cleared his throat, though by the sound of it, he didn't need to.

You've never been to La Scala? Everyone is shocked the first time they go by how narrow and steep and high it is; many are also disappointed. If your seat is anywhere near the front of the orchestra, you have to climb over everyone else to get there. No way around it. She's gotten old, I thought as I waved to Wally Castelbarco. I didn't stop to consider she was already eighty-two.

She stared at me, shook her head, took a step closer, and shook her head again. Volodya's pupil? she finally asked. I nodded. Pardon me for not reacting right away, but you have . . . aged considerably. How's he doing, you ask? I feel no pity for him. My heart always went out to Sonia. A lot of good that did her. My brother-in-law didn't even attend his daughter's burial in our family crypt. The mighty, mighty Horowitz. He should count his blessings I don't say anything . . .

Kaufmann lifted his hands, as if to excuse some behavior, and said, She, too, was Toscanini's daughter, through and through, although . . .

The grandfather clock chimed.

Donati's voice sounded higher than usual. We have fifteen minutes left, so tell me, what lingered?

Pain and happiness. The pain was cheap; let's call it embarrassment. No response whatsoever to the message I had left in person at the Hotel Savoy. As for the happiness?

Thirty-eight years had passed since Carnegie Hall, since the last time I'd seen him. I had avoided the profiles of him on TV, including that feature from '82. To see him briskly approach the piano and give the audience a cursory glance, to get it out of the way, one thing was immediately clear: Horowitz had risen from the grave. His cutaway sat well, and the vest now fit comfortably; there was nothing bloated or puffy about him. He was truly present, as present as those slender hands of his, which packed the same punch they had at age twenty. He sat at the keyboard, body erect and quiet down to his elbows, and demonstrated what virtuosity meant to him: freedom. Do you understand?

I don't, said Donati.

The freedom born of the ability to express anything capable of expression. To transform in a split second from a murderer into an angel and from an angel into a wolf and from a wolf into Maria Callas.

What about Wally, though? What was it she'd wanted to get off her chest?

We should stop talking about him, Kaufmann said.

Donati pulled his legs into his chair and sat there, blanket gathered up to his chin and head resting on his knees, like a sick child. Okay, we'll stop.

Kaufmann closed his eyes. During intermission, he'd been at the bar at La Scala when a woman's voice came from nearby. Well, if it isn't everyone's darling.

Kaufmann had turned around. Wally Castelbarco was craning her neck toward him. Her lips were cerise and smiling. Her eyes—under menacing Toscanini brows, still jet black, even at her age—were not. Everyone's darling. You always were. You have no idea what it's like for a person to spend their entire life vying for recognition and never receiving it. The more fiercely they claim it, the more vehemently it's denied.

She let Kaufmann treat her to champagne and started talking about her sister Wanda. It wasn't just their father who'd dashed Wanda's hopes of becoming somebody. Horowitz, too, had burst her every bubble. No appreciation, no care, no roses or bowing, no complimenting her on a new designer gown, no helping her on with her coat. He had denied Wanda even the most banal of gentlemanly deeds. At the Toscaninis' Riverdale estate, she had once dressed up as Toscanini with a Toscanini mustache and tap-danced on Toscanini's grand piano, making all their party guests laugh. Her father and husband had barricaded themselves upstairs until the applause subsided.

Journalists sneered at the fact that Wanda would jump in to answer questions posed to her husband. She could never have made her voice heard otherwise, Wally Castelbarco said. There were many forms of unsated hunger, but the hunger for recognition would kill you. The countess sensed Kaufmann hanging on her every word, and she awaited a second glass of champagne. She'd meant that literally, she clarified, what she'd said about killing. A sense of humiliation was the reason behind most every war on earth.

Kaufmann clasped Wally's tiny hands and said, *Madonna mia*. The elderly Wally—née Toscanini, married and divorced Countess Castelbarco—spoke steadily, her voice penetrating him. Their father had belittled Wanda, then the same behavior came to define her marriage. Kaufmann was tempted to remind her of how nasty Wanda could be toward Volodya, but then again, they were two armies engaged in trench warfare, both refusing to retreat, both thinking theirs the greater humiliation.

My sister has hardened, but Volodya has too. When people feel humiliated, it's like they've been skinned, so they reach for their armor.

Kaufmann kissed her hand then—no, he kissed both her hands and apologized, without Wally's understanding what for.

In Milan that November evening in 1985, at nearly seventy years old, he finally stopped to consider how Wanda may have felt when, three years after her wedding, her husband gave another man the very look she herself needed.

There he is, said Donati.

The concert hall was vast and brightly lit and filled to the brim with silent spectators in Russian finery. Their silence and their finery seemed at once demanding and detached.

Does he still have family there? Donati whispered.

As you know, he left them all behind sixty years ago. His sister died last year, so he's too late. Nieces, nephews? Maybe.

Horowitz shyly found his way to the podium, patted his treasured grand piano, pressed his lips together, arched his eyebrows as if to make sure he wasn't dreaming, and gazed into the crowd in search of guidance or help. He sat down and launched straight into a piece few there knew, a faraway piece, a piece as far away as Venice: Italian Baroque sonatas, Scarlatti. The camera cut away to faces in the audience as surprise spread through the hall. No one was prepared for the tone that issued forth, fragile and vulnerable and deeply melancholy. The faces were wide open now; nothing could protect them from what was coming.

The two men in the armchairs sat as still as those in the concert hall, as transfixed as the Russian audience by the old man who grew more childlike and blithe with every piece, and who didn't mind the wrong notes he played, because no one else did.

He smiled between pieces, an old conjurer who hadn't lost his touch and whose secrets no one knew.

The words *Rachmaninoff Prélude in G-sharp Minor* appeared on screen. Kaufmann leaned forward, as if then he could hear better. It was almost unbearably beautiful. In the final section, where the melody moves to the left hand, Horowitz crossed his hands to strike the D sharp, which he let hang in space for a full half minute.

Without moving his head, Kaufmann peered at the man beside him, who didn't know what a D sharp was or why the pianist crossed his hands.

Donati sat there with his mouth open, as though four decades had fallen away, and with them, all that had hindered his sense of wonder.

The grandfather clock chimed in the middle of the Scriabin études. Neither heard it.

The grandfather clock chimed in the middle of a Schubert impromptu and a Petrarch sonnet by Liszt, and again, finally, in the middle of the Chopin Polonaise in A-flat Major. Neither heard it.

The time had come for the first encore. Horowitz played a few chords and laughed. He laughed like he might have done in the past, at home with his mother and without fear of anyone forbidding him anything.

Donati rose at the sound of the opening notes of Schumann's "Träumerei."

There he remained until the end, when the camera revealed Horowitz was crying and reaching to the left, where his big white handkerchief lay folded inside the piano, and brushing away his tears and returning the dampened cloth to its place.

Donati switched off the television.

He didn't turn around to face Kaufmann, but addressed the dark square instead.

His fear vanishes when he plays. Is it his fear of death?

Ours is less the fear of death than it is that of not living right, Kaufmann replied.

Was he crying at the thought of everything he's done?

I'd say more likely at the thought of everything he hasn't done. By the way, you could go to Berlin. Horowitz is playing there May 18.

Donati turned around. I'd have good reason to. He's Muslim and lives in Berlin. If I had died, he'd've inherited this house. If his family discovers he's in love with a man, they'll kill one of us. Or both. It's known as an honor killing.

I thought you were planning to die, anyway, Kaufmann said.

It was a quiet night by the lake, and as the blackbirds began to sing, the first warm breeze of the year floated in through the open windows.

Around eight, Kaufmann stood at the driver's side door of his old Peugeot. Donati leaned against the front door frame.

What do you think of my house?

If I were you I'd sell it or give it away. But not to me, please.

Kaufmann opened his car door. As he was about to get in, Donati asked, What was it you wanted to show me, anyway?

Kaufmann straightened, turned back one final time, and said: The possibilities.

LEA SINGER is a German cultural historian and a novelist who uses a pseudonym for her fictional works. Under her legal name of Eva Gesine Baur, she has authored biographies of Frédéric Chopin and Wolfgang Amadeus Mozart. She has also written novels inspired by the lives of pianist Paul Wittgenstein and painter Caspar David Friedrich.

ELISABETH LAUFFER is the recipient of the 2014 Gutekunst Translation Prize. After graduating from Wesleyan University she lived in Berlin where she worked as a commercial translator and then obtained a master's in education from Harvard.

ACKNOWLEDGEMENTS

I WOULD LIKE to recognize those who made this book possible. My thanks to Professor Edith Thauer for her generosity and the insight she provided into Nico Kaufmann's papers, archived at the Zentralbibliothek Zurich. The unpublished fragments of Kaufmann's memoir and the letters he received from Vladimir Horowitz between 1937 and 1939 served as the inspiration for this book and comprise its core. And to my own accompanist—highly musical in every respect and known in plain language as my editor—Cornelia Künne, whose vast expertise is coupled with an ear that detects even the slightest dissonance, a gift one can only dream of as a writer.

THE DRIVE
BY YAIR ASSULIN

This searing novel tells the journey of a young Israeli soldier at the breaking point, unable to continue carrying out his military service, yet terrified of the consequences of leaving the army. As the soldier and his father embark on a lengthy drive to meet with a military psychiatrist, Yair Assulin penetrates the torn world of the hero, whose journey is not just that of a young man facing a crucial dilemma, but a tour of the soul and depths of Israeli society and of those everywhere who resist regimentation and violence.

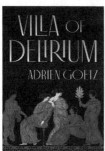

VILLA OF DELIRIUM
BY ADRIEN GOETZ

Along the French Riviera, an illustrious family in thrall to classical antiquity builds a fabulous villa—a replica of a Greek palace, complete with marble columns, furniture of exotic wwoods and frescoes depicting mythological gods. The Reinachs—related to other wealthy Jews like the Rothschilds and the Ephrussis—attempt in the early 1900s to recreate "a pure beauty" lost to modernity and fill it with the pursuit of pleasure and knowledge. This is a Greek epic for the modern era.

AND THE BRIDE CLOSED THE DOOR
BY RONIT MATALON

A young bride shuts herself up in a bedroom on her wedding day, refusing to get married. In this moving and humorous look at contemporary Israel and the chaotic ups and downs of love everywhere, her family gathers outside the locked door, not knowing what to do. The only communication they receive from behind the door are scribbled notes, one of them a cryptic poem about a prodigal daughter returning home. The harder they try to reach the defiant woman, the more the despairing groom is convinced that her refusal should be respected. But what, exactly, ought to be respected? Is this merely a case of cold feet?